KISS OF DEATH

ADAM CROFT

BLACK CANNON
PUBLISHING

First published in Great Britain in 2022.

This edition published in 2022 by Black Cannon Publishing.

ISBN: 978-1-912599-76-9

A CIP catalogue record for this book is available from the British Library.

Printed and bound in Great Britain by Clays Ltd, Elcograf S.p.A.

MORE BOOKS BY ADAM CROFT

RUTLAND CRIME SERIES

1. What Lies Beneath
2. On Borrowed Time
3. In Cold Blood
4. Kiss of Death

KNIGHT & CULVERHOUSE CRIME THRILLERS

1. Too Close for Comfort
2. Guilty as Sin
3. Jack Be Nimble
4. Rough Justice
5. In Too Deep
6. In The Name of the Father
7. With A Vengeance
8. Dead & Buried
9. In Plain Sight
10. Snakes & Ladders

PSYCHOLOGICAL THRILLERS

- Her Last Tomorrow
- Only The Truth
- In Her Image
- Tell Me I'm Wrong
- The Perfect Lie
- Closer To You

KEMPSTON HARDWICK MYSTERIES

1. Exit Stage Left
2. The Westerlea House Mystery
3. Death Under the Sun
4. The Thirteenth Room
5. The Wrong Man

All titles are available to order from all good book shops.

Signed and personalised editions available at adamcroft.net.

Foreign language editions of some titles are available in French, German, Italian, Portuguese, Dutch and Korean. These are available online and in book shops in their native countries.

EBOOK-ONLY SHORT STORIES

- Gone
- The Harder They Fall
- Love You To Death
- The Defender
- Thick as Thieves

To find out more, visit adamcroft.net.

HAVE YOU LISTENED TO THE RUTLAND AUDIOBOOKS?

The Rutland crime series is now available in audiobook format, narrated by Leicester-born **Andy Nyman** (Peaky Blinders, Unforgotten, Star Wars).

The series is available from all good audiobook retailers and libraries now, published by W.F. Howes on their QUEST and Clipper imprints.

W.F. Howes are one of the world's largest audiobook publishers and have been based in Leicestershire since their inception.

W. F. HOWES LTD

QUEST

CLIPPER

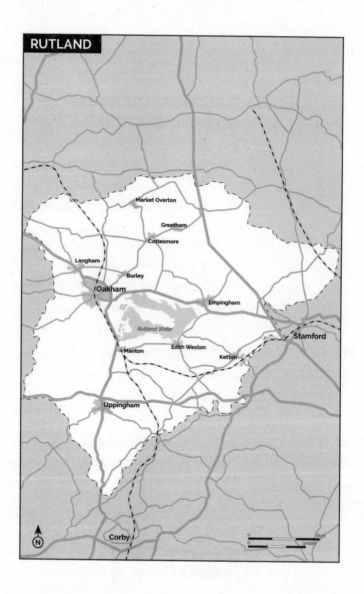

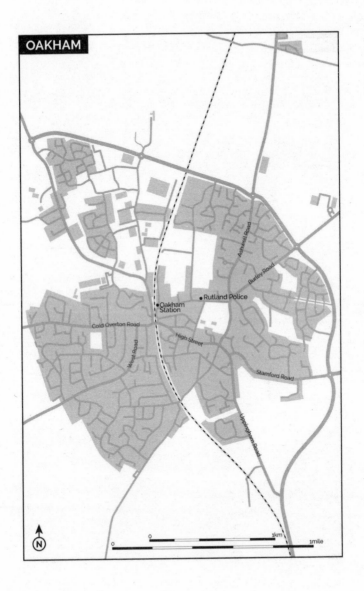

OAKHAM

Ashwell Road
Burley Road
Rutland Police
Oakham
Station
Cold Overton Road
High Street
West Road
Stamford Road
Uppingham Road

N

0   1km
0   1mile

For Ava.

Barbara Patchett winced as she swallowed a chunk of croissant, regretting not chewing it more thoroughly. She poured herself some more grapefruit juice and chugged half the glass, feeling the relief as the croissant dislodged itself from her gullet.

'Brian, are you nearly ready?' she rasped, before coughing to clear her throat.

'Almost,' her husband called from the living room. 'Just trying to sort this last bit.'

Barbara pushed her chair back and stood up from the kitchen table, before taking her plate over to the bin to dispose of the last piece of croissant. As nice as it had been, she'd rather gone off them for the moment.

'I hope you're talking about ironing your shirt, and not that jigsaw puzzle again,' she called.

'I'd have been done by now if they'd photographed

the flipping thing when it was sunny. As it is, the whole bloody lot's grey. Can't see what's a cloud and what's a girder.'

'I'll give you bloody girders if you haven't got that shirt ironed and ready in the next—'

Barbara stopped mid-sentence as her eyes registered two new sights: Brian sauntering into the kitchen in his pyjamas clutching the lid from the jigsaw box, and his crumpled white shirt in a heap next to the toaster.

'Oh, for the love of… Well you'll have to wear it like that now, won't you? You'll just have to go to church looking like Meatloaf.'

'I dunno. I reckon I'd come across more like one of those New Romantics,' Brian replied with a grin.

'Maybe if either of those words actually applied to you,' Barbara muttered under her breath as she washed her hands in the sink before downing the rest of her juice.

'Anyway, the creases will fall out after a few minutes. No-one'll notice under my jacket.'

'That's not the point, is it?' she replied, drying her hands on the tea towel a little more forcefully than usual. 'You're turning up to church in a shirt that looks like a crumpled sheet of paper someone's taken out of the bin. If you'd just listened to what I'd said and ironed it instead of wasting time on that jigsaw puzzle—'

'Well, you try telling the difference between two

shades of grey at this time of the morning. I swear they do it on purpose. I'm telling you they do.'

Barbara furrowed her brow. 'What? Why? What are you talking about?'

'They do it to make you buy more. It's a con.'

Barbara exhaled heavily. 'Will you listen to yourself? It doesn't even make sense. If they wanted you to buy more they'd make them easier to solve, so you get them done and want to buy another one. They wouldn't deliberately make them as frustrating as possible, would they?'

'Well I want to throw the bloody thing out the window. They're certainly not getting any more of my business, that's for sure.'

'Exactly! That's my point. If they wanted to— Oh, for crying out loud, why am I even wasting my breath? Come on. Get your Tony Hadley costume on and let's get moving. We should've left five minutes ago.'

By the time they'd arrived at All Saints Church in Oakham, there was barely a parking space to be found. Eventually, Brian had parked in the Church Street car park, having found a free space hidden amongst the deluge of red Post Office vans. As far as Barbara was concerned, it was an ideal place to leave the car, directly opposite the church and free on a Sunday, but Brian seemed to have an unreasonable dislike for it. It was usually either the spaces or the lanes that were too narrow — sometimes both — but today he just huffed and puffed and muttered under his breath, leaving Barbara to wonder what the problem might be this time.

Secretly, she wondered if he just didn't like coming to church each Sunday. He'd never been a particularly religious man, and she'd long suspected he only came along because it gave him something to do and it didn't cost anything.

She took a long drag of fresh air as she stepped out of the car, trying to fight back the wave of nausea she'd felt over the past couple of minutes. She always felt unwell when she rushed food, and getting herself stressed and worked up was never a situation that ended well. The church had provided a place of refuge for her in so many ways.

They made their way into All Saints and sat down on a pew.

'You alright? You look pale,' Brian said. 'Hope it wasn't my driving.'

'I'm fine,' she replied, looking at his crumpled shirt, which threatened to envelop his grease-splashed maroon tie. 'Just all a bit of a rush this morning.'

'Maybe we should set the alarm for a bit earlier,' he said, oblivious to his wife fighting back a scowl.

'Yes. Maybe.'

By the time the service began, the nausea still hadn't

passed. If anything it had probably got worse, but a growing sense of dizziness and general unease made it difficult to pay too much attention to how sick she was feeling. She was acutely aware of her own heartbeat — something she hadn't often experienced — and wondered if it seemed faster than usual. *It's just indigestion*, she told herself. *Indigestion and stress.*

As the organ started to play and the congregation rose to their feet to sing, Barbara held onto the back of the pew in front of her, feeling desperately unsteady on her feet.

'You sure you're alright?' Brian asked. 'Do you want to go outside?'

'I'm fine,' she replied, her voice hoarse and her mouth dry.

She mouthed along to *When I Survey the Wondrous Cross*, as she did every week with every hymn. She'd always hated her singing voice, ever since her choirmaster at school had told her she sounded like a demented parrot. But she loved the hymns. Just being in the same room as people singing them made her feel ten feet tall. There was something so uplifting, so empowering about the music, the words, the atmosphere. There was nothing else like it on Earth.

As the hymn ended, she sat back down and listened as the vicar spoke, but she found it increasingly difficult to focus on the words. She could hear them, and she knew them, but they just didn't seem to make any sense when put together.

She took a couple of deep breaths, trying to calm her racing heartbeat and push back against the growing and unavoidable sense that her world was closing in on her. She looked around, taking in the details of the church. The organ. The masonry. The bright light — so bright — streaming in through the windows. She squinted, feeling the intense beams searing into her brain, adding to her increasing headache. The floor. She'd look at the floor.

This was her calm place. This was safety. The church had given her so much solace. It had provided purpose and meaning. Especially after everything that had happened.

The congregation rose to their feet again, and Barbara realised she'd barely heard any of the sermon. The sounds seemed duller, more distant. She could just about make out the hymn. *It Is Well with My Soul.* She stood, feeling even more unsteady than she had before, her legs like jelly beneath her.

She went to take another deep breath, but found she struggled. Feeling the panic beginning to rise within her, she closed her eyes and tried to focus on the music, allowing herself to sing and steady her breathing.

'Love, you're not right,' Brian said, taking hold of her arm. 'Do you need to step outside?'

She shook her head, continuing to sing with her eyes closed.

'Love…'

The intonation in her husband's voice made her open her eyes and look at him. He was staring at her lower half. She looked down and saw the tell-tale dark patch growing on the front of her beige trousers.

'Out. I need to get out,' she said, her voice hoarse.

Without waiting for her husband, she shuffled unsteadily along the pew and into the nave, before turning in the direction of the door. As she took her first couple of steps forward, she felt it happening. And she knew at the deepest level of her soul there was nothing she could do.

As the congregation sang, Barbara closed her eyes and fell to the floor.

2

The morning sun warmed the back of Caroline's neck as she clasped Mark's hand, the shingle of Thorpeness Beach crunching underfoot as they walked. Her sons ran on ahead, making the most of trying to play football on the uneven surface, and loving every minute of it.

'This is what you call a Sunday morning,' Mark said, smiling. 'I can't believe how calm it is. I thought it'd be windy on the coast.'

'It's gorgeous,' Caroline replied. 'I bet this beach'll be rammed within a couple of hours, though.'

'I was thinking we could take the opportunity to head down to Aldeburgh. There'll be more for the boys to do there. Especially if the beaches are going to be packed.'

Caroline smiled at Mark. 'Sounds lovely.' For the first time in as long as she could remember, she felt truly relaxed. Moving from London to Rutland had been intended to give them all a clean break, and the irony wasn't lost on her that it was only now, on a beach in Suffolk, that she felt that sense of inner peace.

'You seem much happier,' Mark said, as if reading her thoughts. It'd become clear to her over the past months that she was a far more open book than she'd realised. And where she'd felt the need to close off and keep things to herself, the impression she gave others had been far worse than the open and honest truth.

'I am,' she said. 'It feels like we've come a long way recently.'

'One hundred and twenty-eight miles. And I felt every single one of them.'

'I did say I was happy to share the driving.'

'And you also said I was a terrible backseat driver.'

'That's because you are,' Caroline replied, laughing.

'Then you'll just have to deal with me moaning about the journey, won't you? It's been worth every second, though. Just look at the place. How can you not have your breath taken away by a view like that?'

She'd noticed how much brighter Mark had seemed recently, too. There'd been some dark days after the death of his mother, but she sensed he'd been able to move on in the months that followed.

She wondered if, up until then, he'd felt in limbo, caught between their new life in Rutland and the tie of his mother still being in London. Her own health issues and need to throw herself head-first into work hadn't helped, either, but both of those worries had since disappeared into the background.

Being clear of cancer had lifted a huge weight from her shoulders, and the relative lack of drama at work meant she'd been able to focus more on family life. Although Rutland wasn't historically famed as a centre for violent crimes, it'd experienced a run of major cases that had kept her and her small team working well beyond their means for far too long.

The whole point in moving to Rutland had been for the family to have a fresh start, and for her to work for a police force that wasn't constantly besieged by a deluge of major crimes and chronic underfunding. After years with the Met, she'd certainly seen the appeal of working for a small, rural force in an area with a low crime rate.

Fortunately, it was looking like the run of major incidents they'd had to deal with had just been a flash in the pan. Like any police officer, Caroline would never dare use the word 'quiet' when talking about work, but there was no denying that recent months had been far more relaxed than the ones that came before.

It had meant the world to be able to work reasonable hours without worrying about being called out in the middle of the night. She'd had more time to spend with Mark and the boys, and she'd very quickly seen how that quality time had had such a positive effect on them all. Now, she just needed to keep that going.

'Boys, how do you fancy a little trip out today?' she called.

'Huh?' Archie yelled back, without even looking in her direction.

'I think you mean "pardon". And if you try to stay within a few miles of us, you might actually hear what I'm saying.'

Archie hoofed the ball back in his parents' direction, before he and his brother raced to be the first to reach it.

'I was asking if you fancied a little trip out to Aldeburgh today. It's meant to have the best fish and chips in the country.'

'I love fish and chips!' Archie shrieked.

'And a Martello tower,' Mark added.

'What's that?'

'Kind of like a castle, I guess.'

'I love castles!'

'Fish and chips and castles it is, then. Although I think there's probably one other thing we should do before we head off. I have it on good authority there's a little place up the road here that does rather good ice cream…'

'I love ice cream!'

'Well we'd better get a move on then, hadn't we?' Mark replied, stealing the football with a cheeky toe punt and running off with it, his sons chasing after him with shrieks of delight.

Caroline turned and looked back at the sea, watching as the waves rolled in and washed the shingle before retreating again. She closed her eyes as she listened to it mingling with the sound of the gulls and her own children's ecstasy, and, for the first time in a long time, she felt that all was right with the world.

3

PC Daniel MacLagan looked on as his colleague spoke to another witness at the perimeter around the church. There was always a fine line to tread between preserving a scene and not wanting to cause undue distress to those who'd witnessed a tragic but innocent death.

With both the police and ambulance stations situated mere yards from All Saints Church, the response had been rapid, and it had been confirmed that no-one had left the church in the time since Barbara Patchett had collapsed.

The paramedics had tried in vain to perform CPR on her, but confirmed her dead a short while later. From what Daniel and his colleague had managed to ascertain so far, it sounded as if a heart attack was the likely culprit. Her husband had described how she'd looked pale and seemed unsteady on her feet before collapsing.

It wasn't the first body Daniel had attended, but they didn't seem to get any easier. It was routine for the police to attend when a person died outside of a hospital, in order to be certain no crime was involved before handing the body over to an undertaker.

Daniel's colleague approached him.

'You happy to do COPEGS?' he asked.

'Yeah, can do,' Daniel replied.

COPEGS, yet another police acronym, referred to the reporting of a sudden death back to the control room. Before a sergeant could give authorisation to hand the body over to an undertaker, Daniel would have to give a verbal report on the circumstance of death, other marks or suspicious circumstances, position of the body, examination details completed by a doctor or paramedic and a general health history of the deceased. Only then would the S — supervisor sign-off — be given.

Daniel looked back over his notes, then radioed in to request a call from the control room, which came shortly after.

'Yeah, I'm at the scene of the body at All Saints Church in Oakham. I'd like to pass you COPEGS if that's okay?' Daniel asked.

'Go ahead.'

'We've got a seventy-three-year-old lady by the

name of Barbara Patchett. She collapsed during this morning's church service after appearing dizzy, faint and spaced out. No suspicious bruising or marks visible, but she does appear to have wet herself. Her husband said that happened before she collapsed and was what prompted her to leave her pew and head for the door. She then collapsed in the nave of the church. Multiple witnesses say she looked unsteady, then fell forwards onto the ground. By the time we arrived on scene, CPR had been attempted by a member of the congregation as well as paramedics, who subsequently deemed it unsuccessful and declared her dead. Her general health appears to have been good, although her husband said she tended to be an anxious and highly-strung person and had been on medication to lower her blood pressure, which appeared to be working.'

'All received,' came the response. 'Will get a sergeant to review and call you back.'

Daniel thanked the controller and ended the call, then went back over to speak to his colleague. 'COPEGS passed to control,' he said. 'With any luck we'll be done here soon.'

4

Detective Sergeant Dexter Antoine looked over the COPEGS notes that'd been passed to him by the control room. As the only available sergeant in the area at that moment, the job of supervisor sign-off fell to him.

On the face of it, it seemed a pretty standard death: an elderly woman, presumably a heart attack, but in a rather inconveniently public place. But there was one thing that bothered him slightly.

He read the wording again, this time more carefully. He wanted to make sure he'd read it correctly. He had. The husband told PC MacLagan that Barbara Patchett had experienced involuntary urination before she'd died, and while she was still mobile and lucid. Dexter had known many examples of people losing control of their bodily functions shortly after death — that was perfectly natural — but he wasn't aware of many cases where that'd happened before the person had died. If she'd had some form of stroke, it might have made sense. But that didn't quite match up with the description of her having been on her feet and walking towards the exit of the church between then and collapsing.

There was probably nothing in it, but he had little else to do and the church was barely three hundred yards away, so he figured it made sense to go down and take a look.

It was shaping up to be a glorious day, so Dexter popped on his sunglasses and walked down to All Saints Church, glad he'd picked a light grey suit over a darker fabric. It was starting to look as if spring might already be starting to break into summer.

As soon as he'd crossed the road outside the police station and turned the corner into Church Street, he could see the commotion at the church. He showed his badge to the officer at the outer cordon and made his way towards PC MacLagan, who'd submitted the report.

'Morning. Nice day for it,' he said, employing his well-practised dark humour — something all police officers used to some extent, to deal with the unconventional pressures of the job.

'Not bad,' PC MacLagan replied. 'Might want to get her in the chiller before too long, though.'

Dexter smiled and took off his sunglasses. 'I got your COPEGS. Alright if I take a look?'

'Sure. I wondered if you might.'

'Oh?' Dexter replied, quizzically.

'Well, it couldn't get much more local, could it? And I hear it's been pretty quiet.'

Dexter raised an eyebrow at PC MacLagan. 'Until you said that. That'll have put the mockers on it.'

Dexter stepped into the church, followed by PC MacLagan. 'Is it correct that she pissed herself before she collapsed?' he asked.

'Apparently so. Her husband said he spotted it and mentioned it to her, and that's why she made to leave.'

'Did any other witnesses spot it?'

'No, but there weren't many. Not who were sitting further back than her and would've had her in their eye-line.'

'Maybe they're just a decent bunch of god-fearing folk who wouldn't dare look at a lady's crotch,' Dexter added.

'Maybe. But by all accounts she hit the floor more or less as soon as she'd stepped out into the nave and turned towards the door, so there wouldn't have been much chance for anyone to notice anything anyway.'

Dexter nodded. 'That the husband over there?' he asked, looking in the direction of a distraught-looking gentleman clutching on to a young girl Dexter assumed was the man's granddaughter.

'Him? No, he's the witness who gave CPR. Saw the whole thing happen.'

'So did the little girl, presumably?'

'Yeah. Hell of a thing to see at that age.'

'Have we got someone doing welfare bits?' Dexter asked. In the case of a young child witnessing something as traumatic as a woman dying in front of her, there was a responsibility to ensure no long-term psychological damage was done.

'I put the call in, but they can't get anyone over that quick on a Sunday.'

Dexter sighed. It had never made sense to him that weekend staffing numbers were so often reduced in the police, much the same as they were in hospitals. It wasn't as if crime took a day off at weekends, or people were less likely to fall ill or die.

'I'll do a quick check,' he said, realising PC MacLagan had more than enough on his plate. 'What's his name?'

'God knows,' PC MacLagan replied, flicking through his notebook. 'I've got it here somewhere, though. Fred, I think. Yeah, Fred Barton.'

Dexter smiled. He walked over to the man introduced himself.

'Fred, isn't it? I'm DS Antoine, from Rutland Police.'

'Yes. Hello,' the man replied, his voice quivering as he spoke.

'And what's your name, little lady?'

'This is Tamsin, my granddaughter,' the man replied, blinking heavily as he cleared his throat. 'Sorry. We're both a bit shaken.'

'That's fine. I completely understand. You've given a statement to my colleague, haven't you?'

'Yes. I said I'd give him a call if I remembered anything else, but it's just been such a shock. Everything's a bit of a muddle and a blur, but at the same time I can still see so much of it so clearly.'

'It'll take time to process,' Dexter replied. 'But please don't worry. We've got a duty of care to you, and we'll make sure you get to speak to someone so you can process what's happened in the proper way.'

'Thank you,' the man replied. 'I didn't really know Barbara — only by name — but she seemed such a lovely woman. Always so keen to do the right thing. It doesn't really make any sense.'

'Sometimes these things don't. I know that'll be no consolation at the moment, but if it helps, it doesn't sound as if she was in any prolonged pain or distress.'

The man nodded, and seemed to be a little more reassured.

Dexter spotted PC MacLagan walking a couple of metres away, and stopped him. 'Sorry,' he said to the man and girl, before turning to his colleague. 'Can you show me the husband? I'll need to speak with him.'

PC MacLagan led Dexter back outside and towards a bench, where Brian Patchett was sitting with a uniformed officer, who was starting to go through the traumatic but necessary procedure of completing a sudden death report.

'Mr Patchett? DS Antoine, Rutland Police. My deepest condolences. I understand it's a bad time, but would it be okay if I asked you a couple of quick questions?'

Brian blinked a few times and nodded. 'Yes. Yes, of course.'

The uniformed officer stood up and made way for Dexter to sit and talk to Brian in private.

'First of all, I just wanted to say how sorry I am for your loss. I hear Barbara had been pretty fit and healthy? This must be a terrible shock.'

'Yes. Yes, it is. I mean, she'd looked a bit peaky all morning, but I thought she was just getting flustered as usual. She mentioned feeling a bit sick and dizzy, but I put that down to her bolting her breakfast too quickly before we left the house.'

'Could well be. Did she eat anything unusual?'

'No, just her normal Sunday breakfast.'

Dexter nodded slowly, and tried his hardest not to raise an eyebrow. 'Remind me…'

'Two croissants, a black coffee and some grapefruit juice. She always says that's enough to keep her going through the service, then we tend to pop off and grab an early lunch at the garden centre.'

'Sounds like a lovely way to spend the day. My

colleague said Barbara was on some medication, is that right?'

'Yes. For her blood pressure.'

'Okay,' Dexter said, starting to piece two and two together. 'Do you know what it's called, out of interest?'

'Ooh, now you ask me something. It's got a funny name. I always poke fun at it... Slozem. That's it. Slozem. I used to joke that it helps people's blood pressure because it Slozem down.'

'Very good,' Dexter said, smiling. 'Is it okay if I let my colleague complete the sudden death report with you? I'll be about, and I'll come back and chat with you in a bit.'

'Yes. Yes, of course,' Brian replied.

Dexter stood and walked a little further away before pulling out his mobile phone. He opened the web browser, and typed *Slozem* into the search bar.

He scrolled down until he found the first reputable-looking result that wasn't trying to flog him some drugs online: a page on the NHS website entitled *Diltiazem: a medicine used to treat high blood pressure*. He tapped the link and quickly scanned through the information, before going back to the search bar and typing *diltiazem grapefruit*.

Although he didn't know why or how it worked, he was aware of a common phenomenon whereby grapefruit juice was known to interact badly with lots of medicines, sometimes stopping them working or even leading to dangerous side effects.

One of the first search results was another page on the NHS website, this one entitled *Does grapefruit affect my medicine?* Before he'd even tapped on the link, he read the snippet of text Google had pulled from the website. *Grapefruit juice does not affect diltiazem.*

He tapped through to the website and read the section on calcium channel blockers. It listed eight which interacted poorly with grapefruit juice and could cause serious issues, but the sentence underneath the list was as clear as day. *Grapefruit juice does not affect diltiazem.*

That was one potential cause of death to cross of the list, at least. But something still niggled at the back of his mind. It was the involuntary urination. It just didn't seem to make sense. It wasn't something the paramedics had picked up and mentioned, but then again they'd only arrived a short while after Barbara had already collapsed and died, and they naturally hadn't asked witnesses if she'd wet herself before dying. It'd be perfectly normal for them to assume it'd happened after she'd died, as it so often did.

'You happy for me to call in the undertaker?' PC MacLagan said, appearing at his side.

'Almost,' Dexter replied. 'First of all I just need to make a quick phone call.'

5

The weekly shop wasn't Luke Grennan's favourite chore, but there was no denying that it had to be done.

On the plus side, Sophie appeared to have a natural talent for laying out the shopping list in the same order as the aisles in the shop, no matter how often they were moved around. Although they'd only recently moved in together, he could tell they were going to work well together domestically.

Organising the shopping list in the right order wasn't something that'd ever have occurred to him. He was more of a 'write it down as it occurs to you' kind of man. But Sophie was different. She was different in so many ways.

Her organisational skills had even extended to wedding plans. Although they hadn't yet set a date —

and he hadn't yet officially proposed — she'd already earmarked venues and worked out some potential dates which would minimise financial outlay whilst maximising guest availability. He felt grateful to have someone like Sophie by his side, but at the same time he couldn't deny she put him to shame.

Shame wasn't a new feeling for Luke. He was quite used to feeling inferior, even if he didn't show it on the outside. He often wondered how people saw him, and how that conflicted with the way he felt about himself. He was pretty sure people would describe him as confident, fun-loving and outgoing. At least, that was the image he was trying to portray.

Doing the shopping on a Sunday had been Sophie's routine. Before that, it had been her parents' routine. He didn't mind — he took comfort in that, and he knew exactly where he stood. He'd never had those things. Life had tended to be a little more chaotic. Besides which, it made sense not to be rushing around in the evenings with all the other shoppers, and it meant they always had a well-stocked fridge ahead of another week of work.

He rounded the corner of the baked goods aisle, scanning the shelves for pain au chocolat. That was another great thing about moving in with Sophie. His mum would never have let him eat chocolate for breakfast. Finally, he found the right ones and popped them in the trolley, before scanning down the list for the next few items.

Cleaning products and a couple of bits from the freezer section — they were no problem at all — but it was the last item on the list that threw Luke.

Plus any lunch bits you need for work x

His immediate, instinctive reaction had been annoyance that Sophie hadn't just broken it down into specific items and listed them out in the right order, like she had with everything else, but he stopped himself and reined it back in. That wouldn't be helpful, and he knew it wasn't the real issue. He'd been through all this with Steve, his CBT therapist, and he was now aware that his brain had a tendency to protect itself. It did this by channelling his emotions and frustrations in the wrong way, often misdirecting and misplacing them. He wasn't angry or annoyed at Sophie for not automatically knowing what he wanted for lunch and listing the items in order like he was a child; he was frustrated and anxious because having to do those things himself meant he had to think about work.

Even then, work itself wasn't the real issue. Not at the deepest level. It was the people there, the culture, the buttons they pushed and the deep-seated anxieties they triggered. But he had to work. He had no choice. It was the only way he and Sophie could afford a place together, and there was no other option. He'd experienced life before that. He couldn't go back to the uncertainty and unpredictability of his formative years. Even though the people at work might have triggered his traumas on a regular basis, at least they weren't *actually* them.

It wasn't as if he could just walk out and get another job, either. He'd been lucky to get this one. He had no qualifications, no experience other than labouring. And the culture was going to be the same at any site, with any firm. *That's just how it is*, they'd say. *It's banter.* Luke hated that word. As far as he was concerned, it was just permitted bullying. Calling it 'banter' might have made it sound a bit less harmful and a bit more jokey and fun on the face of things, but the only people having fun were those who were dishing it out. For the poor bastards who had to put up with it, it was anything but. And in his eyes, anyone who needed to joke about and poke fun at other people's perceived faults in order to make themselves appear better, needed to take a long, hard look at themselves. At least, that's what he kept telling himself.

He grabbed the bleach, surface spray and frozen chips, then headed back towards the entrance, where the snacks and lunch bits were kept. He told himself he'd grab a couple of meal deals or some pork pies or something to get him through the first couple of days, and he'd sort the rest out in the week.

He scanned the shelves, not really taking in anything he saw, feeling the familiar tightness in his chest, his teeth clenching tightly, making his jaw hurt. He wiped his face, noticing his hands trembling as he did so.

He glanced over at the checkouts to see how long the queues were. He needed to know if he had enough time to get through. He reckoned if he tried a couple of breathing exercises, he might just make it, but it would be close, and the thought of cutting it too fine was enough to cause additional anxiety in itself.

Without a second thought, he headed for the self-checkouts, judging that he'd get through much quicker.

He ignored the pointed tutting from the elderly gentleman who'd clearly decided Luke had far too many items to be clogging up one of the seven available self-service checkouts, and started to take his items from the basket. He was almost halfway through when he tried to scan the bread, but it wouldn't take. He tried to stretch and flatten the plastic wrapping, before scanning the barcode again, but it failed. He wiped his sweating hands on his trousers, then gave it another go. Still nothing.

Feeling the panic and frustration rising, Luke tapped

the *Finish, pay now* button. Stuff the rest of it, he thought. He'd rather take the flak from Sophie for bollocksing up the shopping than risk a full-on panic attack in the middle of the supermarket.

Fumbling with his credit card, he tapped in his PIN, waited an interminably long time for the checkout to accept his payment and grant him permission to leave, then he grabbed his bags and walked as quickly as he could out of the shop.

Marching through the car park, he kept his eyes on the ground, breathing in through his nose, holding it and releasing the breath slowly through his mouth. He'd managed four by the time he got to his car, flinging open the rear door and dumping the bags on the back seat, before getting in the driver's side and closing the door behind him.

In the quiet and relative safety of his own car, he leaned his head back against the headrest and continued with his breathing exercises, gradually feeling the panic begin to fall. He rolled his shoulders, trying to relieve some of the tension as he felt his hands starting to shake a little less, everything slowly calming until he was almost on a level.

Just as he was about to open his eyes again, a loud knock on the car window made him almost jump out of his seat. It was only the look on the face of the woman who'd knocked which stopped him from falling straight back into panic attack territory.

'Sorry. Are you okay?' she mouthed, with a look of concern.

Luke nodded. 'Yeah. Fine. Thanks,' he mouthed back, with a forced smile and a thumbs up.

He put his key in the ignition, started the car and headed for home.

6

Although the café in Thorpeness Mark mentioned was closed on Sunday mornings, the boys had been pacified by the discovery that Aldeburgh had more than enough ice cream parlours to last them a lifetime.

After parking up, they'd headed to one of the many parlours close to the seafront, and had settled down on the beach, having discovered it to be much quieter than they'd expected.

'Should've gone for rum and raisin after all,' Mark said, taking another delicate lick of his strawberry ice cream.

'Oh, is that one not any good?' Caroline asked.

'Yeah it's fine. But I could've used it as an excuse for you to drive back.'

Caroline laughed. 'I don't think rum and raisin ice

cream would quite be enough to put you over the drink-drive limit.'

'No, but you can't be too careful when there's coppers about. And anyway, I would've just eaten more than enough to make sure.'

'I bet you would. How about you treat yourself to a beer or two with lunch? I don't mind driving back to the B&B. As long as you promise to drink enough to fall asleep the second we get in the car and not be a back-seat driver.'

'Deal.'

Although Caroline and Mark were barely halfway through their ice creams, Josh and Archie had long demolished theirs, and were busy chasing the football around its second beach of the day.

She watched on, amazed at how her sons were able to move about so quickly and ably on the shingle surface. She supposed children just cared less about falling over. Much like a dog, their sole aim was to get to the ball, no matter what it took. They weren't worried about slipping or tripping. It didn't bother them what people looking on might think. They were simply free, enjoying themselves without a care in the world.

As she felt the warmth of the sun on her face, Caroline closed her eyes and tried to remember a time when she'd felt so carefree. She didn't have many clear memories of her childhood. Some were clearer than others, but those weren't always the ones she wanted to remember.

When it came to childhood happiness, she didn't have memories so much as imprints of emotions. Sensory memories. So often, the smell of lavender or hot tar would transport her back, reminiscent of blistering summer days that seemed to go on forever. Six-week summer holidays that lasted a lifetime. A random recollection of sitting on a bus as it passed the supermarket, and feeling blissfully happy, although with no recollection as to why. It wasn't that she had happy memories of bus journeys in general, and she doubted she'd been particularly elated at passing the supermarket in that moment decades ago. She could only assume she must have felt some joyous serenity about something at the time, whether she'd realised it then or not. Or perhaps it was all a trick of the mind, two neural pathways misfiring or getting confused, like an audience member at a hypnotist's show associating somebody whistling with the irresistible impulse to get down on their knees and cluck like a chicken.

She'd only realised she'd started to drift off when she was jolted awake by Archie flinging himself at her for a hug — something neither of her sons did as much now they were getting older, but she certainly wasn't complaining.

'Thank you, darling. What's this for?' she asked.

'Because I love you,' Archie replied. 'And because we get to spend more time with you now.'

Archie ran back over to his brother and carried on their game of football as if he'd just said the most normal and inconsequential thing in the world. For Caroline, though, it had been bittersweet. It was heartwarming to hear how much Archie appreciated her presence and to hear those words, but at the same time it reminded her how much she'd neglected her family previously, without even realising it.

It wasn't the fact work had been busy, nor that she often had to spend long hours in the office. The problem had been her inability to separate her work and home lives, allowing one to infiltrate the other to the detriment of all.

Her phone vibrated beside her, causing her to look down at the screen. It was her colleague, Dexter Antoine.

She felt herself involuntarily clenching her teeth. She knew Dexter wouldn't be calling to see how her holiday was going. It'd be work. A case. She told herself she had no obligation to do anything — she was on annual leave — but she knew it wasn't quite that simple.

'Morning,' she said, answering the call.

'Ah, the squawk of seagulls, the soothing sound of the waves cascading against the shore, the laughter of children frolicking blissfully in the sunshine.'

'You can't pick all that up over the phone.'

'No,' Dexter replied, 'I can't hear a bloody thing. Aidan's brought his new coffee machine in. Sounds like the ten thirty-five to Alicante's taking off from next to the microwave.'

'I'll stick with the crashing waves, thanks. But I'm guessing you haven't called to chat about espressos and lattes?'

'Not this time, but we should definitely schedule that in. Sounds great. I was calling to say we had a woman collapse and die at All Saints this morning. I was asked to sign off on COPEGS, so I thought I'd wander round the corner and take a look. Woman in her seventies, perfectly healthy other than controlled hypertension. She'd been feeling a bit peaky all morning, but started getting dizzy and jittery during the church service before dropping down dead. Inconvenient, but nothing too out of the ordinary, right?'

'Right,' Caroline affirmed, watching her children prancing about in the waves.

'But there's one thing that doesn't quite make sense to me. She'd wet herself. Involuntarily, I mean. Not that anyone would deliberately piss themselves in the middle of a church. Not that early in the morning, anyway. Thing is, her husband said that happened before she died. That's why she went to go outside in the first place. And that was when she collapsed.'

'Did she have any history of doing that before?'

'What, dying or pissing herself?'

Caroline sighed. 'What do you think?'

'Just checking,' Dexter replied with a chuckle. 'And no, apparently not.'

'First time for everything. She's in her seventies.'

'That's nothing nowadays. Certainly doesn't mean you turn into an incontinent vegetable overnight. Just seems really... odd.'

'How was the husband?' Caroline asked.

'Stunned, to be honest. Certainly nothing suspicious on that front, as far as my nose told me.'

'But there's a reason you've called, isn't there?' Caroline asked. Dexter's instincts didn't often fail him.

She heard him sigh at the other end of the line.

'It just doesn't quite seem right. I've been to enough bodies to get a vibe for these things.'

'Paramedics all okay with it?'

'Yeah. Yeah, apparently so. And I know what you're saying. They're the medical experts. But they're not looking at things from the same angle, are they? They ask what they need to know to help her or keep her alive. They're not asking the same questions, not looking at the same things. I mean, let's face it, a woman in her seventies with a history of high blood pressure, who's spent the morning stressed and rushing around, feels a bit off colour, gradually goes pale then collapses and dies — everyone's going to think heart attack, aren't they? They affect women differently. When my nan had one, she said she felt like she had the flu.'

'And what do you think it is?'

'I dunno. Not yet, anyway. But it just seems a little too clean and convenient. And I can't find anything online about involuntary urination during a heart attack. After death, yes. Overactive bladders in heart failure, yes. But not pissing yourself without even realising it.'

'It could be entirely unrelated. Just a coincidence. People can have two completely separate health problems at the same time.'

'I know. But pissing yourself in the middle of church without even noticing, and with no previous history of any form of incontinence whatsoever?'

Caroline sighed again. 'I'm on holiday, Dex.' She caught Mark glancing at her, and she looked back at him. He didn't say anything, but then again he didn't need to.

'I know,' Dexter replied. 'I know. And I'm not asking you to do anything, but—'

'Good.'

'I mean, we've not got a huge amount on at the moment, and it really wouldn't hurt to look into things a bit more, speak to the family, get some background.'

'That's entirely your prerogative, Dex. You're a DS. You can run with that if you think it's the right thing to do and you've got the space to prioritise it.'

'And you don't want me calling you and bothering you about it, right?'

'Like I said, I'm on holiday. And you're a DS. You don't need my authority.'

There was a moment's silence before Dexter replied. 'Alright. Point taken. I'll keep you updated if I find anything, yeah?'

'Don't feel obliged to. I mean it, Dex. You don't need me. You know how to run an investigation. All I'd say is tread carefully. There's a grieving family, and the chances are there's nothing amiss.'

'I know, I know. First rule of any investigation.'

'No, the first rule of any investigation is don't bother your DI when she's on holiday.'

'You must have a newer version of Blackstone's than me, but I'll take the hint. Don't forget to bring me back a stick of rock.'

'Convince Aidan to take the hundred decibel coffee machine back home before I get back next week and I'll bring you two.'

'Deal. Sayonara.'

'Bye, Dex.' Caroline ended the call, and noticed Mark looking at her.

'Work?'

'Yeah. Just Dex getting his knickers in a twist again. He seems to forget he's perfectly qualified to do all these things himself. Sometimes I wonder how he manages to get dressed in the mornings without calling me to check which tie I think looks best.'

Mark smiled and reached over, taking her hand. 'Thank you.'

'For what?' Caroline replied, smiling back.

'For looking at things that way. For dealing with it like you did. I really appreciate it. Just wanted you to know that.'

Caroline squeezed her husband's hand and looked back over at Josh and Archie, who were happily screeching as they chased the waves back down the beach, then sprinted away from them each time they returned. She felt the warm sun on her face, and the even warmer love from her family, and basked in it, hoping it would overwhelm her uncomfortable urge.

7

He sat in his car and watched. He'd never been particularly good at lip reading — especially not at this distance — but he could pick up a lot through body language. Not that anyone wouldn't be able to decode the shaking, heaving shoulders of a man who'd watched his wife die earlier that day, speaking to two police officers in the living room of the house he and his wife had shared for so many years.

It was a sort of morbid curiosity that had brought him here. The commotion at the church that morning had been an eye-opener, to say the least.

He'd kept himself in the background, for the most part, confused and conflicting feelings running through him. He'd wondered if there would be a sign. He supposed there had to be. Otherwise, how would he know? It was all very well for God's will to be done, but what use would it be if it wasn't known?

He'd often questioned the omniscience of God. Omnipresent, yes. There could be no physical place left untouched by His presence. He felt Him everywhere. Omnipotent, certainly. God's power was indisputable in both reach and gravity. He'd experienced that, without doubt. But omniscience? He wasn't sure. Could God truly know all? And even if He did, would He make his own knowledge known?

These were the thoughts that kept him awake at night, no matter how much they hurt his head. After all, it was human nature to ask questions. To find reasons. To seek justice. And he'd had more reason than most to chase all those things.

Of course, the human impact couldn't go unnoticed. He could see it now, right in front of his eyes, as Brian Patchett recalled the horrors he'd witnessed only hours earlier, now indelibly printed on his mind for eternity. He knew what was to come for Brian. He'd been there. He'd wake in the night, shaking, dripping with sweat. He'd see her face in the bathroom mirror, obscured by steam and wishful thinking. He'd read an article in the newspaper and lift his head to read a section out to her, before realising she'd never hear.

He was only human himself. Expecting not to feel empathy was like asking a banana not to be yellow. But that didn't — couldn't — override the power of God, nor the awe he felt at having seen it enacted before his very eyes.

It was real. It was true. Whatever human emotions presented themselves, this was so much greater. He'd seen His power, right there in the house of God. The Lord had answered him, and He had done so in the clearest way possible.

He felt justified. He felt vindicated.

He had been absolved.

8

Dexter was cautious not to overstate the planned exploration into the circumstances surrounding Barbara Patchett's death. He didn't want to call it an investigation — he knew there weren't the grounds for that, and he didn't want to cause unnecessary distress to Barbara's family — but he did feel it warranted looking into a little more closely, just to make sure.

He sat down with Detective Constables Sara Henshaw and Aidan Chilcott, as he often did on a Monday morning, to discuss any updates or progress from those who'd been working the weekend.

'I had an interesting one yesterday,' he said, suspecting he might have overdone the casual tone and given the game away immediately. 'I attended the scene of a sudden death. Seventy-three-year-old Oakham woman by the name of Barbara Patchett. She collapsed during a church service at All Saints, after feeling a bit unwell beforehand. We've not exactly been snowed under recently, so I wondered if we might be able to have a little nosey around without alerting her loved ones.'

'Suspicious circs?' Aidan asked, his eyes narrowing.

'Not that I can put my finger on,' Dexter replied, bending the truth a little. 'More of a general sense of things not quite adding up. She'd wet herself, for example. But not after she'd died. The husband reckons that'd happened while she was in the middle of singing a hymn and that's what made her go to leave the church. No history of incontinence, apparently, so it's a bit of a coincidence for it to happen the first time just seconds before she dies, isn't it?'

'It does sound a bit strange, but is it suspicious?'

'I reckon so,' Dex replied. 'My sister's a palliative care nurse. Last year she was doing a lot of work on an initiative into signs that people are approaching death. Basically, they realised they were spending a load of money propping up people who it wouldn't make a difference to. She didn't stop going on about it for months. That was one of the things she mentioned — that they either slow down or stop urinating completely, or develop incontinence.'

Aidan looked at Sara, then back at Dex. 'So why's that suspicious? Sounds like it's entirely as expected.'

'I think he means those changes would happen

gradually over days, weeks or months,' Sara said. 'Not in the thirty seconds before death.'

'Exactly that,' Dex replied. 'It might be nothing. Just a little something making me feel uneasy, that's all.'

'Probably that tie. It's giving me a headache, too.'

'Very good. In any case, I've specifically requested toxicology from the post mortem, and stomach contents analysis. The coroner's in a good mood and has signed that off, so we'll wait to hear back. Now, I got a bit side-tracked yesterday afternoon, but I did get round to running Barbara and her husband through the PNC and they're clean, but there is reference to a son, Ross, who's got a fair bit of history to say the least. His parents have an active non-molestation order on him.'

'Well that seems like a good place to start,' Sara said. 'Do we know the terms of the order?'

'Yep — no letters, texts or other communications other than through a solicitor, and no coming within one hundred metres of Barbara and Brian's house. I've not got round to taking in the detail, but from what I can gather there was a pattern of increasingly threatening behaviour from Ross towards his parents, which appears to be the result of years of heavy drug use. It looks like he rocked up at the house one day and did a number on his dad, then followed up with a text threatening to kill them both.'

'Lovely guy,' Aidan said. 'Anything else on his record?'

As Aidan spoke, Sara looked across the desk at him. She'd been keen on Aidan for quite some time, but had never plucked up the courage to mention it to him or ask him out. She'd been on the verge of doing so a few months earlier, only for Aidan to reveal that his boyfriend had just left him. Assuming he was gay, Sara had pushed her feelings back down, only to later find out Aidan had started a new relationship with a woman called Keira, who he'd been with ever since.

Keira seemed nice — unfortunately. Sara hated herself for saying it, and she loved to see Aidan happy, but she couldn't deny there was a part of her that hoped Keira would do something really appalling so Aidan would dump her and leave the door open for Sara.

She was used to being on her own, but she yearned for company. She'd been adopted as a baby, her birth parents having been addicts and criminals. Even though her adoptive parents had been wonderful in so many ways, the knowledge they weren't strictly related had always left a small gap in Sara's heart. With her birth parents now dead — her mother only recently — that particular gap was one that would never be filled, yet she'd always felt that some form of deeper connection with another human was not only possible, but sorely lacking.

'Put it this way,' Dexter replied to Aidan. 'The only reason I didn't print out Ross Patchett's PNC record was my concern for the rainforest. Almost all logged by

Leicestershire, so he's kept off our radar for the most part. He lives in the city, and seems to cause enough upset over there, so they can keep him. There's nothing on him that's been logged in Rutland since he decked his old man.'

'Good job, too. Like you say, they can keep him. I imagine he'll be tagged or tracked if he's that well known. Can't be too hard to find out if he's been over this way at all recently. Surely someone would've said if he'd been at the church, though?'

'Well, yeah,' Dexter replied. 'There's nothing suggesting he was, but we definitely need to rule it out. Besides which, he might not have needed to be. If he'd mucked around with her medication or something, he could've caused the damage weeks ago. She might've just happened to have collapsed in church through pure chance.'

'Either that or he was hiding at the back with a poison dart,' Aidan joked.

'Mmmm. Maybe he dressed up as a paramedic or a vicar so he could remove it before anyone noticed. Very Miss Marple. Although I did have half a thought that the dad might be covering for him, but I scrapped that idea pretty quickly.'

'Yeah, I can't see it,' Aidan replied. 'If you've had to take out an injunction against someone banning them from coming within a hundred yards of your property, you're not going to cover for them if they bump off your missus, are you?'

'It sounds like we might be getting a bit too far ahead of ourselves anyway,' Sara interjected. 'Especially if there aren't any signs Barbara's death was suspicious, other than the fact her son has a record of violence.'

'And specifically threatening to kill her,' Aidan added.

'True, but people make those sorts of threats all the time, and people die all the time. It doesn't mean the two are connected. But like you say, we're not exactly rushed off our feet at the moment so it'll be something to do.'

Dexter chuckled. 'That's the spirit. We should put that on a motivational poster or something. Everybody clear on what needs doing?'

Sara and Aidan nodded.

'Good stuff. Let's crack on then, shall we?'

9

Although the forecast for the rest of the day was good, it had been a chilly start to the morning for Luke Grennan. He was working on a site in Edith Weston that week — as he had been the week before — and he knew he'd spend most of it looking forward to the weekend.

As well as it meaning he wouldn't have to go to work, he and Sophie were going to a wedding fair at the NEC in Birmingham. It had been Sophie's idea, of course, but he was very much looking forward to it. He wouldn't tell any of the guys at work that, though. Not in a million years.

He took another long swig from his drink bottle before getting out of his car at the last possible moment whilst still being on time, and headed onto site. He'd been trying to take in a lot more water recently, in an

attempt to feel better, look better and improve his
mental health. He couldn't stand drinking water itself,
though. Too boring. Initially, he'd taken on most of his
liquid through tea and coffee at work, but that stopped
when he found a butt plug at the bottom of his cup of
darjeeling. It'd been bad enough that they'd taken the
piss out of his choice of drink in the first place, but
using a buttplug to hammer home Luke wanting milk in
it? Too much.

For now, it would have to be squashes, fruit juices
and whatever else he'd managed to get hold of. After
yesterday's disaster at the supermarket, he'd had to grab
a couple of bottles out of the fridge — some organic,
artisan fruit juices Sophie had bought at a boutique
health foods shop, no doubt hand-squeezed by a
Rwandan mountain gorilla before being sieved through
the underpants of a small orphan child. Still, if it made
her feel better.

She'd been very clear she wanted to lose weight for
the wedding, which was a concept that struck Luke as
odd. He could well understand anyone wanting to lose
weight in general, or even so their partner would find
them more attractive, but he couldn't quite get his head
around her wanting to lose weight specifically for the
one day everyone *else* had to see her. Still, he was sure he
was probably looking at this in the wrong way, as he
tended to do, and as Sophie tended to tell him he did.

'Morning gay boy,' Jonesy said as Luke got out of

his car. He'd been working with Jonesy for over a year, and he still had no idea what his first name was. There was a good chance Jonesy didn't, either.

'Morning,' Luke replied, his headache already starting to build, as it had been all morning. Stress, he told himself. Stress and anxiety.

Jonesy pointed to his drink bottle. 'What you got in there? Spunk?'

'Juice.'

'Cock juice?'

'No, just juice.'

'Suit yourself. Gaz is upstairs. He wants to see you in private, apparently. He's got a girlfriend, though, so don't get too excited.'

'I know. So have I.'

'Yeah alright then.'

Luke put his drink bottle down on a table, then made his way towards the stairs and up to find Gaz. As he took the first few steps, he noticed his balance starting to wobble and his vision blurring slightly. His anxiety sometimes gave him odd symptoms, but nothing quite like this. Still, after yesterday's panic attack and the pressure of coming in this morning, he knew he had to give himself a bit of leeway on that front.

He reached the top of the stairs and walked over to his boss. Gaz was one of the reasons he'd stuck with the job. Even though he was a bit of a pillock when he was with the rest of the boys on site, he knew when to tone it down and was professional enough on a one-to-one basis.

'You alright?' Gaz asked as Luke walked over. 'You're looking a bit pale.'

'Yeah, I just feel a bit off this morning.'

'Off?'

'Yeah. Kinda sick.'

'Late night?'

'I wish. Probably just coming down with something.'

'Do you need to go home? Might not be safe for you to be here if you're feeling that bad.'

'I'm alright. I'll be fine.'

'Mate, you're sweating like a paedo in a playground. Don't worry about the other lads. I'll tell them I've sent you off to size up a new job or something. I won't tell them you've gone off ill.'

Luke wished he could believe that. 'Honestly, I'll be alright in a minute. Jonesy said you wanted to see me about something. Seemed important.'

Gaz shook his head and chuckled. 'He's an absolute wind-up merchant. I didn't say anything of the sort. I had a word with him yesterday about keeping his crap to a minimum when we've got other contractors and suits and stuff walking about, so he's probably just getting it all out of his system now before they turn up.'

Luke felt his heart hammering in his chest as his vision began to narrow. Strange, he thought. It didn't feel quite like the usual panic attack. In any case, this wouldn't be the sort of thing to set one off. If anything, finding out Jonesy had wound him up again would usually make him angry or annoyed, but this time he felt... He didn't know how he felt.

The only way he could have described it was that it felt like the world was turning in on him. His body felt like it was giving up. As he tried to make sense of it all, he heard the sound of steel-toe-capped boots jogging up the stairs, accompanied by Jonesy's familiar snicker.

Before he'd even realised what was happening, Luke's legs gave way and he fell forward.

Gaz's reactions were quick, and he put out his arms to take Luke's weight, lowering him slowly to the ground, before leaning across and putting him in the recovery position.

'Christ alive, I didn't know you were both at it!' Jonesy said, his laugh becoming a bellow. 'I leave you two alone for ten seconds...'

'Will you pack it in?' Gaz yelled back at him. 'Make yourself useful for once, will you, and call an ambulance.'

10

As far as Dexter was concerned, it was typical that a case had cropped up within an hour of asking Sara and Aidan to look into Barbara Patchett's death. The new case would have to take priority.

Whereas Barbara Patchett's circumstances had simply not sat right with Dexter, this new death had been categorised as suspicious by default, due to the deceased's age and health.

Based on what he'd been able to gather from the initial call, the dead man was just two weeks off his twenty-fifth birthday, and had been perfectly fit and healthy — until he'd keeled over at work that morning. Although paramedics had been called and thought they'd had him stabilised, he'd died in the ambulance on the way to hospital.

Attending sudden deaths wasn't a part of the job

any police officer relished, but there was no denying
some were worse than others. Although it sounded
harsh, it was true to say the death of an elderly man or
woman was far less distressing than that of a teenager
or child with their whole life ahead of them. Dexter
could see why that was, and why most people's
instinctive reaction was similar, but it wasn't something
that ever sat comfortably with him. It wasn't that he
disagreed; his innate response was exactly the same.
And that's what made him feel so uncomfortable. After
all, a life was a life, and anyone's death left a hole, both
in the lives of their family and loved ones, and in the
fabric of the universe.

As he arrived on site, Dexter parked his car,
switched off the engine and stepped out, meeting a
uniformed constable at the entrance.

'Morning. All secured?' Dexter asked, confirming
the scene had been cleared and preserved. It was a mere
formality, because no scene was ever truly preserved. He
already knew paramedics had been traipsing through —
quite rightly, from the deceased's point of view — as
well as other people who'd been working on site and in
the vicinity when the young man died. Of course, it
wasn't possible to press the pause button on the world at
the moment of death, but Dexter couldn't disagree it
would be much more helpful.

The main worry was the contamination of evidence.
This could come in many forms, and none of them

made the police's job any easier. Attempts at resuscitation tended to mean moving, or at least handling, the body. Injuries caused during CPR could be difficult to distinguish from those which happened in the lead up to death. People trying to help the dying person would inevitably leave their DNA at the scene, whereas they otherwise wouldn't. All in all, a large part of the early stages of an investigation — particularly from a forensic standpoint — involved trying to establish precisely what had happened.

Dexter had attended scenes where a body had been found hours after death. He recalled one particular incident where a disabled woman in her fifties had died. She'd been found in her living room by a neighbour, who swore blind she was sprawled on the floor next to her coffee table when he found her. The officer who attended alongside Dexter believed this account. But on looking more closely at the body, Dexter noticed the skin was much darker — almost bruised — around the woman's lower back, buttocks, feet and ankles, and the backs of her upper legs. He knew this lividity was caused by the blood pooling at the body's lowest points after death. It was gravity in action. The lividity on the woman's body indicated to Dexter that she'd been sitting down in her armchair when she'd died. The neighbour later admitted he knew the woman — who lived with various mental health conditions — kept her life savings stuffed down the back of her armchair. He'd discovered her dead in the chair and, without further thought, placed her on the floor, raided and pocketed the cash, then called the emergency services.

In most situations, a far greater story was told after death than before. Where a person had been dead for a while, the strict and immovable laws of nature marched on, without pesky human intervention. If someone had only recently died, it often — perhaps paradoxically — became much more difficult to determine what had happened, and when. Regardless, the golden hour was still considered such, and the first twenty-four hours of an investigation were sacrosanct.

As the uniformed officer led Dexter onto the site and up the stairs to where the man had collapsed, he briefed him on what they knew.

'Twenty-four-year-old male, by the name of Luke Grennan. He's been working on site as a labourer all last week and this week. His boss, Gary Cracknell, was with him just before he died. He said Luke had seemed a bit unwell, but he just seemed to turn suddenly and collapse. There was another chap, goes by the name of Jonesy, who came up the stairs just after Luke collapsed. He's with an officer downstairs.'

'Lovely, thanks,' Dexter replied. 'I'll give you a shout if I need anything.'

Dexter looked over at a man in his mid-forties, who was sitting on a stack of wooden planks, staring at a space on the floor. A female officer was standing next to him, and Dexter nodded that she could leave.

'It just don't make no sense,' the man said, almost to himself. 'What the hell happened? I can't figure it out.'

'Are you Mr Cracknell? I'm Detective Sergeant Dexter Antoine from Rutland Police. I'm really sorry to hear about your colleague. Did you know him well?'

'Well enough. Quiet lad, but stuck it out. Worked hard. Been with us a while. I just… I just can't.'

'I realise how upsetting it must be, and how shocked you are. And I'm really sorry to do this, but I do need to ask you some questions. It's important we do it now, while everything is still so fresh in your memory. I hope you understand.'

Gary Cracknell swallowed, blinked a few times, then rubbed his eyes. 'Yeah. Yeah, course. I owe it to him, don't I?'

Dexter forced a smile. 'I'd say so. Can you talk me through what happened this morning? From when you arrived, right up to the moment Luke collapsed.'

Gary took a deep breath, let out a heavy sigh, and began to speak.

'I got here about half-seven. I ask the lads to arrive for eight. Luke's always the last one. I think he times it to arrive bang on, but he's never late and always works hard, so I don't mind. Jesus Christ. Sorry. It just keeps sort of hitting me, you know? That he's gone.'

'It's okay,' Dexter said. 'Take your time.'

Gary sighed again. 'I was up here, getting some bits prepared and trying to plan ahead, making sure we'd be done and dusted by Friday afternoon. We've got a big job starting next week, and I knew it'd be tight here, so I was going to check who might be available Saturday in case we ran over. No bloody doubt about that now, is there? Sorry. I know that's not helpful. I shouldn't have said that.'

'Honestly, don't worry. You've got a lot going through your mind. None of our brains ever know how to cope with something like this, so it's perfectly natural for it to do some weird and wonderful things while it's processing what's happened.'

'You should be a counsellor, not a copper,' Gary said.

Dexter smiled. 'Trust me, the two aren't a million miles apart. So, you were up here, planning ahead for the week.'

'Yeah. Sorry. I was up here, and I heard a few of the lads coming in downstairs and just getting on with things. I could hear Jonesy — you can always hear Jonesy — but I didn't really pay much attention to what they were saying. Laughing and pissing about as usual. I told them they needed to pack it in while other people were about, because we're not the only ones on site and it don't look very professional, you know? I mean, I don't want to stop anyone from having fun, and this ain't a sweatshop, but it's not right in front of other people. Anyway, about eight-ish, Luke comes up the stairs. I guess he'd just arrived. He says Jonesy told him I wanted to speak to him.'

'Okay. And how did he look? How did he seem?'

'Not right,' Gary replied. 'Not right at all.'

'Can you be a bit more specific?'

'He just looked sort of... I dunno. Pale. Clammy, maybe. He seemed a bit agitated, but at the same time sort of woozy and not with it. If it was one of the other lads I would've thought he'd been on something, but that ain't Luke's style. I thought maybe he'd had a heavy night out, but he reckoned not. Anyway, we've all had hangovers that've killed us, but not literally.'

Dexter raised one corner of his mouth into a small smile. 'Fortunately not,' he said.

'So he says to me Jonesy said I wanted to talk to him, right? And I just said I didn't — not really — and that Jonesy was on the wind-up again. I mean, I did speak to the others about not dicking around on site, but I didn't need to say anything to Luke because he always got on with the job anyway. But yeah, he seemed really off. Just not with it. I told him he should go home, because he wouldn't be much use here if he could barely stand, and I needed him fit and well for the rest of the week. I was trying to get him to go back home and rest, and that was when he just sort of went.'

'Went? Can you describe what happened?'

'Yeah, his eyes just kind of glazed over a bit. Like

something had switched off inside, you know? They were just… there. Like he'd stopped seeing, but his eyes were still there. I mean, obviously they were. You know what I mean.'

'I think so,' Dexter replied.

'I was about to tell him to sit down, 'cause I thought he was passing out or something, but it seemed like more than that. I dunno. I still can't really describe it. Then he just kind of fell forward, but down, like his legs had gone. I put my arms out to catch him so he didn't hit the deck and hurt himself, and I put him in the recovery position. Well, I think I did. It's been ages since I did any training like that. I used to be a first aider at the football years ago, but it's all gone now. I really hope I didn't do it wrong. There isn't a chance I… you know… is there?'

'I don't imagine so, no. I really wouldn't start thinking things like that. If anything, it sounds like you saved him from causing himself more damage on the way down.'

'Yeah, well, I dunno how anything could've caused him any more damage than killing the poor git.'

'I know. You did the right thing, though. So, he's collapsed, you've caught him, lowered him to the ground and put him in the recovery position.'

'Or at least what I thought was the recovery position, yeah.'

'And what happened then?'

'I was trying to work out what to do, trying to remember the training, but panicking. About that time, Jonesy came up the stairs being a prat as usual, giving it all that and making fun, saying I'm trying to bum him or something, and I just shouted at him to call an ambulance.'

'And was it Jonesy who called?'

'Yeah. He had his mobile on him. He was up here with me when he called, and he stayed here.'

'Did anyone else come up?'

'No. Bloody lucky, too. I told Jonesy to stay by the top of the stairs so no-one came in. Didn't want them seeing this.'

Dexter nodded, an uneasy thought starting to form at the back of his mind. 'What was Luke's health like?' he asked. 'Did he have any pre-existing conditions at all?'

Gary curled his bottom lip over and shook his head. 'No, not that I knew of. He was always fit and healthy. You see all the stories in the news, don't you, about young lads who keel over on the football pitch or something. Usually some undetected heart problem that was never spotted. But usually they're absolutely fine, then they just kind of go, you know? That's not how this was. You could see he wasn't right and he was obviously in a rough way. He said he felt sick and he looked dizzy, but he wasn't clutching his chest or anything. A good mate of mine had a heart attack at his mum's birthday party a few years back, and it didn't look anything like this. She never forgave him for that.'

Dexter smiled. 'I'm sure he's very sorry. Is Jonesy around? I'd like to have a quick chat, if that's alright.'

'Course,' Gary replied. 'Think he's round the back, talking to one of your colleagues.'

Dexter thanked Gary and left him with the uniformed officer, then went off in search of Jonesy. The shock was palpable on the faces of Luke's colleagues as Dexter walked past them downstairs. It was a familiar look — one he'd seen many times before. It was the sudden realisation that life was all too short, and that any normal, run-of-the-mill day could very quickly turn into something unexpectedly life-changing.

He passed Luke's colleagues, setting off in search of Jonesy, who he found outside the back of the building, being half propped up, half comforted by a uniformed officer.

He looked like he'd been crying, his eyes red and his cheeks stained with tears. A puddle of vomit had started to trickle its way down the gradual incline of the paving.

'Detective Sergeant Dexter Antoine, from Rutland Police. Really sorry to hear about your colleague. Is now a good time to have a quick chat?'

Jonesy closed his eyes and nodded silently. The uniformed officer headed back inside, leaving them on their own.

'Sorry to be blunt,' Dexter said, 'but do you mind if I ask you your name?'

'Jonesy,' came the instinctive response.

'Sorry, I mean your full name. We need it for the report.'

Jonesy sighed, then looked behind him, making sure his colleagues were out of earshot. 'Cornelius Percival-Jones,' he said through gritted teeth.

Dexter nodded and managed to stifle his grin. 'Got a middle name?' he asked, even though it wasn't strictly needed other than for his own amusement.

'Hildebrand. Don't ask.'

'Your secret's safe with me. I presume you'd prefer it if I called you Jonesy?'

'You can call me sweetheart, for all I care. I've spent my whole bloody life trying to hide that name from people.'

'Never considered changing it by deed poll?'

Jonesy shook his head. 'Money in the family. I mentioned it once when I was a teenager and let's just say it didn't go down well. I wouldn't get a penny if I did that to them. They're already embarrassed enough that I didn't go into finance or become a stockbroker like my brothers. Not all that fun when you're heavily dyslexic, hate school and love rebelling against your parents.'

'Except when their inheritance is involved,' Dexter replied with a wry smile.

'We've all got our limits. I'm hardly expecting this gig to carry me through my twilight years.'

'Probably fewer dead bodies on the floor of the Stock Exchange, though?'

Jonesy thrust his hands into his pockets. 'Don't you bet on it. Difference is they either hang themselves or get coked up to the eyeballs and have a massive heart attack on top of some exotic hooker. I mean, if you had to choose… Not that I'm joking about it, of course. Not with… you know.'

'It's alright. Don't worry. I get it. Are you okay to talk about it? It'd be good to ask you a few questions while it's still fresh in your memory.'

Jonesy nodded. 'Yeah. Yeah, I'll do my best. I mean, I don't really know anything, to be honest. Luke turned up, I made some joke about Gaz wanting to see him, so he went upstairs, I went up just after and he'd collapsed.'

'Okay. Let's roll back a bit to when Luke came in. How did he seem?'

Jonesy shrugged. 'Alright, I guess. I mean, maybe a bit rough now I think about it, but he's usually a right grumpy sod anyway, so I didn't really pay much attention.'

'A bit rough how?'

'I dunno. Sort of pale. Tired. Not quite with it, you know?'

'Alright. And do you remember what you said to each other?'

Jonesy took a hand out of his pocket and rubbed his head. 'Just messing about, really.'

'How so?'

There were a few moments' silence. 'I think I called him gay or something like that.'

Dexter raised an eyebrow and nodded slowly. The man's uneasiness told him everything. 'Okay. Can I ask why?'

Jonesy shrugged. 'Just the sort of thing you do in this job. Banter, ain't it?'

'I wouldn't know. The only times I ever come across homophobia is when I'm charging people with hate crimes.'

Jonesy looked at Dexter, a sudden flash of fear crossing his face. 'No, it definitely ain't that. It's not like that. Luke's not even gay. He's got a girlfriend and everything.'

'That wouldn't make a difference. But in any case, it's not what I'm here for. I'd rather talk about what happened this morning.'

'I dunno,' Jonesy said after a few seconds. 'I told him Gaz had been looking for him and wanted a word. Said it sounded serious. I was just messing about, though. Winding him up, you know?'

'Was that something you did a lot?' Dexter asked, sure he already knew the answer.

Jonesy shrugged again. 'Like I said. All part of the job, really. If you don't join in with that sort of thing you won't survive five minutes round here.'

'And did Luke join in?' Dexter asked.

Jonesy swallowed. 'That's not what I meant. It's just a turn of phrase, you know?'

'I know. I was just asking if Luke tended to join in.'

'Not really. I mean, never, to be honest. He didn't really like all that stuff. Christ, seems so weird talking about him like he's not here anymore. I mean, I know he isn't, but still.'

Dexter could see the shock painted on Jonesy's face, and thought twice about mentioning workplace bullying. 'Did Luke go straight upstairs after you said that?' he asked.

'Yeah. Yeah, he did.'

'And did you hear what was being said?'

Jonesy shook his head. 'Nah, too much noise going on down here, and I wasn't really listening. I gave it a minute or so, then I went up to watch the carnage. I mean, you know, I thought Luke'd be all confused and stuff and that it'd be funny. I didn't mean I expected him to be… you know.'

'I know. So talk me through what happened when you went upstairs.'

'Well, I went up. I think I was probably laughing. I got to the top of the stairs and there's a sort of studio space, and I could see Luke had collapsed. Gaz was lying him down and trying to put him on his side, so it must've only just happened literally a second before.'

'How did Gaz seem?'

'Shocked. Really shocked. And then when I saw Luke's face, you could just tell it wasn't good. It didn't look like he'd passed out or anything. He looked sort of… gone. Hard to describe, really. Gaz shouted at me to phone an ambulance, so I did. He started doing CPR and stuff, but there was just nothing happening. Then when the ambulance got here, they had a go and they reckoned they'd got him stable enough to move, but by the time they'd got him into the ambulance he'd gone again. One of the lads went with him and called us from the hospital to say he hadn't made it. Absolutely mental. Just couldn't believe it. I don't suppose they've said what it was, have they?'

'Sorry,' Dexter said, shaking his head once. 'It'll be a little while before we know that. They'll want to examine him and look at all that in their own time. I know it's tough not knowing.'

Jonesy shrugged. 'It's alright. Just wondered, you know? He always seemed so fit and healthy. Makes you want answers, don't it? Trying to make sense of it, and all that. Scares the life out of you to think it can all be over just like that. You never know, do you? Any one of us could be walking around with some heart defect or a brain tumour or something like that. You could be a few minutes from death and not know about it. Doesn't bear thinking about. Sort of thing that makes you want to just live your life. All that time we spend worrying about stupid stuff, which school to put the kids into, what colour to paint the bathroom. Then you jog up the stairs and that happens. Christ.'

Jonesy was right. It wasn't unheard of for young people to die suddenly and unexpectedly. But from a police point of view, it always had to be treated as suspicious until they knew otherwise. And bearing recent events in mind, Dexter couldn't avoid the growing sense of unease starting to build within him.

11

Caroline ended the call and put her phone back in her pocket. She looked around her, trying to gauge just how far she'd walked. She'd been able to tell from Dexter's tone at the start of the call that this wasn't going to be quick, and that it wasn't a call she'd have wanted to take in front of Mark and the boys.

On the face of it, it was just a coincidence. Not even that, really. Two deaths in the county in just under twenty-four hours wasn't all that rare. People died. It happened. But it was odd that both Barbara Patchett and Luke Grennan had died suddenly and unexpectedly whilst going about their normal daily lives, and that neither of them had been particularly ill.

Their post-mortems would reveal more, of course. She'd told Dexter as much, even though she knew he already knew that. She also knew she was trying to convince herself as much as she was him — just as she had been when she'd jumped on their medical histories.

Police had already spoken to Luke Grennan's fiancee, who'd revealed he'd been prescribed anti-anxiety medication and had been actively trying to bring down his stress levels. But Dexter was right: they were nowhere near the sorts of circumstances that'd cause a young man to suddenly keel over and die. An undiagnosed heart issue alongside that? It was possible. She didn't know how much screening doctors did before prescribing medication like that.

She'd also jumped on the revelation that Barbara Patchett had been taking medication to lower her blood pressure, as if that might explain things. But again, Dexter had been right: the meds had been successful, and regular GP checkups showed her blood pressure had been kept perfectly within normal range.

Caroline had always been the first person to run with a hunch. It had rarely been proven wrong in the past. Often it had been slightly skew-whiff, and on occasion the significance had only become apparent much later, but her hunches had rarely been without merit. And Dexter knew it. She could hear the confusion — almost disappointment — in his voice as she'd told him she didn't think there was anything to warrant an investigation, and that she certainly wouldn't be cutting her holiday short for two sudden but non-suspicious deaths. But who needed to deem them suspicious?

The truth was it only needed one police officer to decide that something didn't quite add up. And when that officer was a Detective Sergeant, he had every right and expectation to open a case and to investigate fully. She hadn't told him not to — she wouldn't — but she knew deep down that the more importance she placed on it, the less she'd be able to resist getting involved.

More than that, Dexter would want her there. He'd need her there. It wasn't that he was incapable — far from it — but the structure of Rutland Police and the nature of the county's low crime rate meant they were severely under-resourced when it came to major crimes. It wasn't usual for a Detective Inspector to get personally involved in cases, speak to witnesses and take control of the day-to-day business unless the investigation was particularly complex, but they didn't have much choice. Their small team struggled at the best of times, and it was often a case of all hands to the pump when a major case landed on their desks.

Caroline wondered how long it'd be before they'd have to stop using the excuse that their low funding was caused by low crime rates. Her team had certainly had a busy couple of years. Besides which, despite the fact that no-one wanted higher crime rates in their area, even fewer wanted police funding to be cut. Sooner or later, though, it was inevitable that conversations over increased resources would need to be had.

She'd asked Dexter to give her a few minutes, and said she'd call him back. She wanted — needed — the thinking time, but she also knew Dexter would take her answer as final. This way, it would seem less like a rash decision, and would absolve her from having to worry about it for the rest of her holiday.

Things had been so positive with Mark and the boys recently. She'd put so much effort into making sure they felt they were her priority, rather than the job. And they were. Of course they were. But the job was a necessity. It wasn't just a matter of finances, either: Caroline felt a deep drive to get justice for those who'd been victims of major crimes, and that need to do the right thing in the face of unspeakable evil was something she knew she could never ignore. At the same time, though, she couldn't let it get between her and her family. She'd seen so many police officers' marriages and relationships fall apart because of it. The old maxim about being 'married to the job' wasn't just a saying. It took over every part of your life, and it wasn't just the obvious issues like the long, unsociable hours. It had more subtle ways of creeping in.

There were the officers who slept with cricket bats under their beds, or who felt unable to drink in certain pubs, visit particular areas or who became distinctly uneasy every time female members of their family left the house. Although most people were aware of some of the crimes that went on, either through reading the newspaper or seeing things on TV, the vast majority went completely unreported. And that was before consideration of crimes that'd been prevented, or potentially violent criminals who'd been kept just about on the straight and narrow, constantly teetering on that line, who could easily fall onto the wrong side at any given moment. Caroline often thought that if most people realised how close they lived to criminality, they'd never leave the house.

Despite the high levels of crime in some areas, most people didn't consider the fact that even serious criminals didn't spend all their time committing serious crimes. Every car thief walks past countless cars every day, and doesn't steal the vast majority of them. Rapists don't attack every woman they see. Burglars are perfectly capable of passing a house without breaking into it. So what made them cross the line when they did? And how could anyone possibly know they were going to be the next victim of crime?

Car thieves sent their children to school, and would be waiting by the gate at the end of the day with everyone else. Rapists ate in local restaurants and drank in local pubs. Burglars shopped at Tescos and Sainsbury's like every other member of society. And how often did anyone consider that those people were around them all the time, doing the same things they were doing?

On the other hand, she knew public paranoia would cause more harm than good. The facts remained: car thieves walk past most cars, rapists walk past most women and burglars walk past most houses. Not only that, but most people weren't car thieves, rapists or burglars. Most people were inherently good, and fuelling paranoia would have its own serious consequences. She'd seen the harm the 'us and them' mentality had on society. Indeed, it had directly caused many crimes in itself, from racist attacks to football hooliganism, and even burglary and fraud. The thought that 'they're different', 'they can afford it' or 'they'll be insured' was driven by division.

These were the thoughts that kept Caroline awake at night. And, like any other police officer, she knew that although you could leave the job, the job would never leave you. Those understandings and realisations were things that never went. You couldn't un-see them. The only option was to learn to live with them, to deal with them in the best way possible and to try as hard as you could to not let it affect the rest of your life, even though you knew damn well it would.

But it didn't need to affect her marriage and her family. Underneath it all, Mark understood the job. He respected it. He knew what it involved on a psychological level. For him, it was more about the time

Caroline spent in the office, away from him and their sons. Things had been different when she'd been in uniform, and even when she'd been a DC. The hours were still long, but they'd been a known quantity. There were shift patterns and reliable annual leave, and everybody knew where they stood. As she'd climbed the ladder, those lines had become blurred, and the move to Rutland had blurred them even further. Here, she had an added sense of responsibility. Although the crime rate was much lower than it was in London when she'd worked for the Met, she didn't have the same resources to rely on. And, when all was said and done, the family of a murder victim in Rutland was no different to the family of a murder victim in London. Both were hurting the same. Both had their lives turned upside down. Both needed justice.

Although life and work were generally easier in Rutland, when a big case landed it was so much harder than it had been in London. That wasn't easy to explain to her family, either, especially when they'd moved to Rutland to escape the stresses of the metropolis and to live a calmer, simpler life together.

Perhaps she'd wanted the best of both worlds. Maybe she'd genuinely believed she could balance the two in a way that would work. But ultimately she knew what was important to her. She'd always known deep down, but the past few months had put it right in front of her eyes. She'd felt almost guilty at not having seen it before, and having neglected it. But there was no use looking back. The only way was forward.

She took her phone back out of her pocket and called Dexter. He answered within two rings.

'Dex, it's me,' she said. 'I've had a think about it, and I don't think we need to do anything drastic. Keep doing what you're doing. Use what you've got. Sara and Aidan are there, so you've got enough manpower to speak to friends and family, draw links, see if there might be something there. There probably isn't, so I don't think we need scale things up. We don't even know there was foul play involved in either of the deaths, and at the moment we've got nothing more than your hunch. I'm not discounting that, of course, but it doesn't mean we can just throw everything at it, either. It could just be a complete coincidence. They might both have had some sort of sudden medical event. It happens. We'll know more after the post mortems. In the meantime, keep doing what you're doing, and let me know if you find anything, alright?'

Dexter was silent for a couple of moments. 'So you're not coming back?'

'I'll be back in a few days anyway. You'll be fine. Like we said, it's probably nothing. I imagine by this time tomorrow we'll have it confirmed they'd died of a stroke, or a sudden heart attack or a brain haemorrhage or something like that.'

'What, both of them?'

'It happens. Could just be a roll of the dice.'

'She pissed herself in the middle of the church, boss. She was a perfectly healthy woman. She wasn't even that old.'

Caroline rubbed her forehead with her free hand. 'There'll be a reason. And it'll probably be completely innocent. Like I say, by all means speak to the family, but don't make your suspicions known. Gather information. We don't need to use a sledgehammer to crack a nut.'

'And if it's not a nut?'

Caroline swallowed. 'Then we'll find out soon enough, won't we?'

12

Faith Pearson felt the familiar burn of lactic acid building up in her muscles, and in a strange way it felt good. It'd been a while since she'd been able to get out on a proper run, but she knew if she could just break through this wall, she'd be able to push on and get a good session in.

The burn didn't used to start this early, she was sure of it. Then again, she was out of practice. Her recent injuries had set her back far more than she would readily admit, and she knew she had to do something to stop the inevitable rot, which would only get worse with inaction.

Faith was the first person to admit she needed to be a regular runner. She liked to party, she liked to drink and she liked to eat rubbish. If she wasn't exercising, the weight tended to pile on, making it even harder to get going if and when she finally did get the motivation or an injury-free period.

She'd heard people talking about a 'runner's high'. She had a theory about that, and it was a simple one: that it was absolute bollocks. Her teenage years had taught her plenty about getting high, and spending a Monday evening punting it round the back streets of Oakham in a pair of Hi-Tec trainers wasn't it. The sort of people who talked about a 'runner's high' were the type who got high when they accidentally took a second dose of paracetamol after three hours instead of four. They were the ones who got a 'real chilli kick' out of upgrading their chicken korma to a tikka masala, or started tripping balls whenever there was a new episode of *The Archers*. To Faith, running was merely a necessity, borne out of the reality that she knew how to have a properly good time.

She couldn't deny there was an element of fun in trying to beat her own personal best, or syncing her watch with her phone and finding out she'd burnt more calories than she'd eaten. Maybe that was the data analyst in her. Either way, there was no way she'd be spending her evenings out running unless she absolutely had to.

She'd bought a treadmill a couple of years back, with the intention of being able to run at home. Faith knew her limitations, and cold winters would be one that'd give her a good excuse not to run outside. And besides, she could get her exercise in whilst watching Netflix or catching up on the telly she'd missed over the weekend. That'd been great for about three days, until the people in the flat below complained about the noise waking their newborn baby. She'd been tempted to mention that she hadn't been all that chuffed with said sprog waking her up with its wailing into the early hours, but she'd been too stunned by the father's description of Faith's exercising. To be fair to him, he hadn't known the noise was caused by her running on a treadmill, but phrases like 'a herd of demented wildebeest' hadn't done much for her self-esteem.

So she'd sold the treadmill to a friend (who didn't have downstairs neighbours) and bought herself an exercise bike. She'd made sure to read the reviews carefully, searching for words such as 'noisy', 'loud' and any reference to wild plains animals. To be fair, the research had been worthwhile, because the bike was almost completely silent when in use. The only time it was more silent was when it had inevitably become a makeshift clothes horse, which is how it had spent the majority of its existence. If there was one unfortunate necessity of her existence Faith hated more than exercise, it was washing. It wasn't even the washing part that was the problem, either: it was the whole chain of horrendous events it put into play. Shoving the clothes into the washing machine, popping in some powder and pressing a button? Fine. Trying to remember which clothes in the pile next to her bed had been worn once and which had been worn for three months solid, separating whites from colours, working out which spin cycle to use and whether she needed bio or non-bio, remembering to actually switch the bloody thing on when she wasn't asleep or at work and likely to find a load of musty washing three days later, hanging it and drying it, ironing the selection of clothes which were simply not designed to be ironable yet looked horrendous unironed... Giving up and chucking it all on the exercise bike had been a far more attractive proposition, and it meant she had yet another excuse not to break a sweat.

She rounded the corner of a residential street and smiled inwardly, the burn in her legs starting to ease a little. It would be much easier from here on in, especially if she could maintain a steady rate and control her breathing. If she could just get herself into a nice coast, there was a chance she'd be able to put in a decent time. It wouldn't be anywhere near her best, but it'd almost certainly be far better than she might have expected under the circumstances.

She glanced down at her smartwatch, taking in the array of readings and numbers on the screen. Her heart rate was higher than she would've liked, but she supposed she shouldn't be surprised. In any case, keeping it high would ensure she stayed in the cardio zone, according to one of her apps. Although this zone was more effective at building heart health and efficiency rather than losing weight, a stronger heart would give her a better platform for those longer, slower, fat burning and fitness runs that'd come later.

Her mouth was dry, which was unusual. She tended to down a pint or two of water before a run, which had dual benefits: it meant she wouldn't get too thirsty while she was out, plus she'd run the return leg at a record pace in order to get back to use the toilet. She cursed herself for having swerved the water this time in favour of some juice she'd picked up on her way home from work. It was meant to be a last little treat to herself — a symbol that her revamped and revitalised exercise routine didn't *technically* begin until she'd taken that first step onto the pavement and started running.

It had been a bad move — there was no doubting that now. She didn't know whether it was the sudden sugar rush wearing off (what *did* 'no added sugar' mean in a drink that was full of natural sugars?) or her digestive system not being particularly keen on half a litre of citric acid sloshing about inside it, but she'd definitely stick to water next time.

Now she thought about it, her mouth had been feeling a little dry before she'd left the house. She'd had some of the juice an hour or so earlier, and had been feeling fine until then. Everyone knew these drinks manufacturers added stuff that made you want to drink more — even if they did claim to be organic and freshly squeezed. She should've stuck to water, she told herself. No-one ever got thirstier after drinking water.

She decided to slow the pace a little. It wouldn't do her any good to lose more fluid, especially with her heart hammering the way it was. She needed to bring it down.

Knowing her chances of posting a reasonable time had passed, Faith slowed to a fast walk, then a slower walk, before a growing sense of dizziness and nausea began to take over.

Not long left now. She just had to get home.

At the end of South Street, she made her way onto the footbridge over the railway line, taking the steps two at a time on the way up, and one at a time on the way back down onto Braunston Road.

She stopped at a low wall outside someone's house and and sat down, taking deep breaths to try and bring down her heart rate. The more she tried to slow her breaths, the harder it became — an increasing desperation as she started to gulp at the air, frantically trying to take in more oxygen without panicking herself and making things worse.

She didn't know whether the dizziness had taken over first, or if it had been a lack of oxygen, or perhaps even her heart giving up. She barely had a second or two to consider that final thought, before the tarmac pavement came rushing up to meet her.

13

It was a rare treat for the boys to be allowed to stay up late. Caroline and Mark had always been keen to stick to routine, and they'd never wanted to be those parents that let their kids stay up until nine or ten in the evening, then wondered why they were horrible little monsters all the time. Even when Caroline had been working late, Mark was assiduous in ensuring the bedtime routine was stuck to. If anything, he'd been stricter about it than she had. But tonight was different. Tonight was their wedding anniversary, and they were all celebrating together.

Admittedly, it was more through necessity than anything. Mark having booked a holiday over their anniversary had been a lovely idea, but it had left them with limited options. They couldn't ask someone they knew to babysit, because they were hours from home.

Grabbing a takeaway or some bits from the local shop and eating back at their accommodation didn't quite have the requisite romantic ring to it either. Their only option had been to book a nice meal out and bring the boys along with them.

Thankfully, Josh and Archie tended to behave well in public, and Caroline had often felt blessed not to have been cursed with the badly-behaved tearaways she'd seen some parents having to deal with. In any case, they were getting older now, and it was a genuine pleasure to be able to share the evening with them.

Mark had booked a table at a gastropub a few miles outside town — the sort of place that smelled of freshly sawn wood, cooked steak and spilled wine, with a heavy top note of Glade air freshener. Secretly hoping someone at the next table had ordered fried onions or something laden with garlic, Caroline sat down at the round table, across from Mark and with one of her sons either side of them.

'Nice and cosy,' she said, peering across yards of open table towards her husband and wishing she'd brought her long-distance glasses.

Mark raised a hand to his ear and scrunched his face as if he couldn't hear her, then smiled. 'Can't knock it for its romantic vibe, can you?'

'Romantic?' Caroline replied. 'I think it'd be better described as contraceptive.'

'What does that mean?' Archie asked, tuning in to

the conversation at the least opportune moment — a talent all children seemed to be born with.

'Just that it's pretty big. We have to shout across the table, because it's so huge,' Mark said.

'Good evening,' a young waitress said, gliding over to their table with a rictus smile. 'Are you ready to order some drinks?'

'Mr Chambers is a contraceptive,' Archie said, wistfully picking up and reading a menu. 'He's my maths teacher.'

The waitress raised an eyebrow.

'Bottle of red wine and two orange juices, please,' Mark said.

'Okay… We've got a Malbec, a Pinot Noir, a—'

'That'd be lovely.'

'Which one?'

'Er, the second one. Thank you.'

The waitress forced a smile, took a quick glance at Archie, then headed back towards the bar area.

'How are you going to explain that one?' Caroline asked, trying to stifle a laugh, once the waitress had gone.

'I'm not. I'm going to pretend it never happened. She misheard him.'

Caroline snorted, amused at her husband's mild discomfort.

'Are we going to get escorted out by Social Services or something now?' Mark asked, only half joking.

'No, of course not,' Caroline replied, watching Mark's face relax. 'Mr Chambers might expect a visit, though.'

Mark looked up at her.

'I'm joking. It's fine. Kids say stuff, Mark. In any case, it'll give us a dinner party anecdote for years to come.'

Before Mark could reply, they were interrupted by the sound of Caroline's phone ringing. She looked at the screen, and saw Dexter's name on it. She cancelled the call.

'Sorry. Thought I'd put it on silent,' she said. 'Anyway. Shall we have a look at the menu? She'll be back in a minute to ask us what we want. Just as soon as she's off the phone to Child Protection. Do you reckon the fish is caught locally?'

'I don't like fish,' Josh chimed.

'Don't order it then,' Caroline replied.

'I want a burger.'

'Good. Order a burger then. But maybe with a "please" on the end.'

Caroline looked at Mark, who'd also heard her phone vibrating in her pocket, against the chair.

'You might as well answer it,' he said. 'It might be important. And if it's not, you can tell them where to go.'

'Are you sure?'

'Yes. Take it.'

'I'll be telling him where to go anyway,' she said, pulling the phone from her pocket and standing up. 'He's got to learn to think for himself. Back in a mo.'

Caroline stepped outside to take the call. The air was still warm, and would be for some hours.

'Dex,' she said, answering the phone. 'We're just out for dinner. It's our anniversary. What's up?'

Any hopes Caroline had of this heading Dexter off at the pass were quickly dashed.

'Sorry, boss. But I think we've got a real problem.'

Caroline closed her eyes. 'Go on.'

'We've had another sudden death. A young woman out for an evening run in Oakham, found dead on the pavement on Braunston Road, by the footbridge over the railway.'

The significance wasn't lost on Caroline. Although she knew nothing about the woman who'd died, Dexter had already described her as young, and the fact she'd been out for a run made it likely she was at least fairly fit and healthy. She'd be hard pushed to argue this could still be a terrible coincidence.

'Right. What else do we know?' she asked, feeling the tension in her own voice.

'Not a huge amount. I'm at the scene now. Uniform called it in. She hasn't got any ID on her, as she'd been out for a run. She wasn't carrying a phone, but she was wearing an Apple Watch, which makes it unlikely she was mugged. No signs of any injury or external trauma other than where she hit the floor, by the looks of things.'

Caroline sighed. She knew what this meant. 'Okay. Thanks. Get the watch bagged up. They'll be able to get an ID from that and link it to the owner. Those things track your heart rate and all sorts, so it might even help us paint a picture of what happened. We'll be able to rule out a sudden heart attack or anything along those lines, and it might even lead us towards a cause of death.'

'Already done,' Dexter replied. 'It's on its way to the computer boffins as we speak.'

'Alright. Good. She'll have a family at home. Loved ones. Someone'll notice she's missing before long, and we'll be able to join the dots. Anything of interest from the paramedics?'

'Not really. Nothing useful, anyway. One of them was on shift yesterday and attended to Luke Grennan. She made a comment about it being unusual to get two like that, so close together. Nothing on a medical front, though. I suppose from their point of view they couldn't see any obvious cause or anything they could treat. They always seem to be just that bit too late to be able to do anything about it. Not their fault, of course. Nothing that can be done.'

Caroline sighed again. That was one of the things that had concerned her most: that it seemed nothing could be done. It wasn't normal for fit and healthy young people to drop dead in the street and to be beyond medical help by the time an ambulance arrived.

The logic was fast becoming immovable. If coincidence and freak medical phenomena were to be discounted, the only answer was that something — or someone — else was killing them. With no obvious marks or trauma to the victims, very few possibilities remained.

To her, it seemed increasingly likely they were looking at some form of poisoning. The key would be the link between the victims. Why had these people been chosen? Or was it purely random? Perhaps they'd somehow been caught in the crossfire, much like the poor police officer who'd fallen prey to the Russian nerve agent attack in Salisbury a few years earlier.

Caroline tried to shake the thought from her mind. It wouldn't do anyone any good for her to run away with crazy theories of Russian spies roaming the streets of Rutland. As with most things in policing, the simplest and most obvious explanation was usually the right one.

'I'm going to open this as an official investigation,' Dexter said, as if reading her thoughts. 'We need to make sure we've got the resources allocated to it, especially if it's what it looks like. Christ, if this is random then we're in for a ride. What if there's more? Who knows who's going to be next? It could be anyone.'

Caroline glanced back at the restaurant, and at the smiling faces of her family seated around the table in the large bay window, happily engaged in what looked like a three-way game of rock, paper, scissors.

'There'll be a link or a pattern,' she said. 'There always is.'

'I hope so,' Dexter replied. 'Because if it's purely random… Well, it doesn't bear thinking about.'

Caroline swallowed and nodded, even though Dexter couldn't see her. It hadn't taken long for her world to turn.

14

The rest of the anniversary meal had been more than a little subdued, even though Caroline had tried her level best to maintain a brave face and not let developments back in Rutland spoil their evening.

Although the boys were blissfully unaware and were just pleased to have been allowed to stay up late, as ever there was no fooling Mark. Sometimes, Caroline wished her husband didn't know her quite as well as he did, and she was well aware he'd have pieced together the phone call from Dexter and her subsequent demeanour and figured out almost exactly what had been said.

His face and body language seemed to veer between concerned and hurt: concerned for her that something serious had clearly happened, and hurt that she was once again letting her work get in the way of their family life. She knew Mark would bring it up the moment the boys were in bed, and she only hoped that by then he'd settled on concern as his primary emotion. No matter what else, the last thing she wanted was to hurt anybody.

On any other evening, it'd be a relief to say goodnight to her sons and settle down with Mark and a bottle of wine, but she had a feeling it wasn't going to be quite so relaxing this time — despite the occasion. As she opened a bottle of red, she decided to take control of the situation.

'That was Dexter on the phone earlier,' she said, pouring two glasses.

'I guessed it might've been. Why do I sense it was a little more than calling to ask for your advice this time?'

Caroline tensed her jaw and took a breath. 'Because it might need a little more than advice. Something big's happened. Happening, in fact. People have died.'

'What, you mean like an accident?' Mark asked, his voice hopeful, yet not entirely.

'No. Not like an accident. At least it's not looking like it at the moment.'

'So what, how many people are we talking? Do you mean one event? Different ones? Some kind of cover-up?'

'No, nothing like that. I know I'm being cryptic, but you know I can't tell you details that aren't already in the public domain. I'm not trying to hide anything from you. I just… I just can't.'

'I know. I appreciate that. I just meant it might be nice to have a bit more of an idea as to what's so important to get in the way of your family holiday and our anniversary. I want to understand.'

Caroline shook her head softly. 'I know you do. And trust me, I want you to understand.'

Mark stayed silent for a few moments.

'You want to go back, don't you?' he said, finally.

'I don't *want* to, no.'

'But you're going to.'

'I don't know,' she said, before wondering why she hadn't just told him the truth. 'I might have to. We're such a small team, when something like this comes along I don't really have any choice.'

'Of course you have a choice,' Mark said, with a heavy sigh. 'You've always got a choice. You're entitled to your holiday. Legally, if nothing else. And if the team's too small to cope with its workload, that's for the higher-ups to sort out. More resources, more funding, whatever. That's not for you to worry about, Caz. Not every problem in the world has to become your personal responsibility. It's just a job.'

'It's not just a job, Mark. It's protecting the public. I've got a duty, especially when people are dying. And the team isn't too small to cope. Most of the time we're overstaffed if anything. It's rare these sorts of things come around, but when they do—'

'Yeah, well it's not seeming all that rare,' Mark said,

interrupting her. 'If it was rare, we wouldn't have to keep having these conversations, would we? It's our anniversary, Caz.'

'I doubt very much that's something that will've crossed a killer's mind, to be honest with you. I don't like it anymore than you do. And anyway, I'm not going anywhere tonight,' she said, taking a step towards him and putting her arms around his waist. 'I want tonight to be just how we wanted it to be. Tomorrow's another day.'

Mark gave a small nod. 'So you'll be going back tomorrow?' he asked, his eyes dull.

'We've only got a few days left. I'll have a word and arrange to get the time back. And more. We can get two holidays out of it. It won't be the end of the world.'

'Okay. Alright, well we'll all come back. That way it won't seem so weird.'

Caroline shook her head. 'No, no don't. The boys'll be upset. They're loving it here.'

'They love that you're here. It won't be the same if you aren't. They'll understand. Anyway, Josh keeps going on about how much he misses Kayden. Maybe we can sell it to him that they get to have an extra couple of playdates, eh?'

Caroline smiled awkwardly. 'Honestly, I think it'd be safer if the three of you stayed here until we were meant to come back anyway. I'll get a train back, so you guys still have the car.'

'A train? That'll take forever.'

'If I get a cab to Ipswich and time it right, it'll be about three hours door to door. No different to driving.'

'You actually looked it up?'

'Of course I did. How else was I going to know?'

Mark looked at her. 'Safer?'

Caroline cocked her head. 'What do you mean?'

'You said "safer". It'd be "safer" for the three of us to stay here.'

'Okay, better. Easier.'

'That's not the same as safer. Tell me what's going on, Caz.'

'I can't.'

'Can't or won't?'

'I can't, Mark. I would if I could.'

Mark wrinkled his brow and picked at his hand. 'Should we be worried? I mean, I know you say you didn't, but you definitely said it'd be safer here. Are we in some sort of danger? Has someone made a threat? I need to know that, at least. For the kids. We need to keep them safe.'

Caroline shook her head. 'No, it's nothing like that.'

'Then why the urgency? Why can't we come with you?'

She considered this for a few moments, her head caught in a whirlwind of conflicting thoughts and emotions.

She gave a half-hearted shrug. The truth was she

couldn't guarantee it *was* safe. There seemed to be very little anyone knew right now, and she had even less of an understanding while she was halfway across the country.

Caroline had always disliked people who claimed others 'just didn't understand' when they actually just hadn't bothered explaining, but she'd found herself thinking those exact words more and more over the years. Any work in the public sector tended to be difficult for others to relate to, but that effect was amplified in certain professions. She'd had friends who were doctors and nurses, and — of course — plenty who were police officers, and there were things that others couldn't ever understand.

How could you explain the completely indescribable smell of a dead body that's been found in a warm flat three weeks after taking its last breath? No matter what anyone imagined, it wouldn't come close to the reality. It was a stench that permeated every fibre of your being, and clung to you for hours and days later, like bleach fumes in your nostrils. It embedded itself in your olfactory system, giving you whiffs of reminders long after the smell had actually gone. And it wasn't just a bad smell. It wasn't even a stench. There simply was no word to describe what it was. It was on another level — a deeper one — that seemed to awaken every dark reflex within you. Caroline supposed it was innate — an instinctive biological red flag that all human beings were programmed to find utterly, deeply repulsive. And she supposed there was good reason for that, on an evolutionary level. The smell of death meant danger was near. If our caveman ancestors came across a decaying fellow human, the likelihood was predators were around. Whether a tiger, bear or rival tribesman, the cause was irrelevant: human biology simply needed to provide an instinctive repellant that would keep the rest of the species well away and far from danger.

But it wasn't even about describing smells. That wasn't the sort of thing that'd drive people apart or create a chasm in a relationship. Sometimes there were single cases or events that turned a person, but more often than not it was a build-up of incidents that caused a larger problem. Attending your first dead body was traumatising. Your next few were desensitising. And all subsequent ones were destabilising. The problem was, no-one ever spotted the point at which they'd moved from stage two to three. Although the initial shock and revulsion faded into the background, the accumulation of profound stressors could be crippling. And more often than not, you wouldn't realise until it was too late.

It was a job that changed you. It had to. There was no other way. If it didn't, you wouldn't be able to do it. And if your mind and self weren't deeply traumatised by the things you had to see and deal with on a daily basis, there were a whole host of other ways you'd suffer. No-one could understand that absolute drive for justice until they'd looked into the eyes of a mother who'd just lost her son.

Caroline remembered one case early on in her career in the Met, where she'd had to break the awful news to a woman that her fourteen-year-old boy had been stabbed and killed in a gang-related incident. He'd hardly been a gangster, either, and was simply sitting in a park with some friends of a friend. He'd had no way of knowing what those older lads were involved in, and his mother had been even more blissfully unaware. She'd sent her boy off to school, expecting him back in the evening, and the only knock at her door had been from a young police officer, speaking words that would make her entire world fall apart. She could still picture her face now. It wasn't something she'd ever forget. It was imprinted on her mind, and always would be. Like the smell of death, it was indescribable — and rightly so.

She'd delayed her decision to have children by a good two years after that. And even when she'd been pregnant with the boys, there'd been a deep-seated fear — a guilt, almost — that she was bringing them into a world she knew was unsafe. It had always been her drive to make it safer, to get justice for those who had fallen victim to its evils. To provide some closure, some legitimacy — *something* — for the families and loved ones left behind. For that boy's mother, and all the other boys' mothers who'd come after. And that was the most devastating and destructive realisation of all: that there would be more. There would always be more.

Amongst her colleagues over the years, she'd seen countless marriages dissolve. Two people who began their relationship as close as could be, driven apart by the unavoidable abyss the job would open up between them. Once one person had seen such darkness, the void between them would never be closed. Some kept it covered up. Others ignored it. But it always had an effect, and that effect was always damaging.

Even now, as she spoke to Mark, she realised she could never explain. She knew there was no way he could ever understand why she couldn't just lie on a beach or sit in a café — no matter how beautiful or relaxing — when there was a chance she could stop another family experiencing that destruction. At the very least, she could get answers for those who already had.

'I really thought we were getting somewhere, Caz.'

Caroline closed her eyes. 'We were. We are. It doesn't mean we've thrown all that away and gone back to square one just because I have to go into work once on my day off. There's a big case and I'm needed.'

'It won't just be once, then, will it? And it's not just a day off. You're cutting short a family holiday. The first one we've had in ages. Tonight's meant to be our anniversary.'

'And it still is. Look, I'm not going to stay there. It

could all be done in a few hours. I'll head back, oversee what's going on, make sure Dex knows he's in charge and I'll talk the Super into drafting in more bodies. Then I'll come back and we'll enjoy the rest of the holiday. We don't need to let it ruin our evening. All the more reason to make the most of it, eh?'

Mark narrowed his eyes. 'Make the most of it? You want to "make the most" of our anniversary night? Wow.'

'You know what I meant,' Caroline replied, sensing there was no way of coming out of this conversation positively.

'Yeah. Yeah, I think I did. And that's what worries me. This is why I wanted you to leave your phone at home, or block all work calls while we were away.'

'It doesn't work like that, Mark.'

'Of course it bloody works like that! That's exactly how it works. It's just a job, Caz. It's like any job. You have work time, then you have family time. Holidays are family time. I thought we'd talked about all this? God knows how many hundreds of times.'

Caroline lowered her head. 'Maybe I should just go now. We're obviously not getting anywhere with this, and if it's only going to spoil your evening having me around I might as well get back and get some sleep before the morning.'

'The trains won't be running at this time of night.'

'I'll drive. I'll be back tomorrow night, if not the day after.'

'You can't. You've been drinking.'

'I had one glass of wine at the restaurant.'

'You stuck to one glass so you'd be legal to drive back, didn't you?'

'No, I stuck to one glass because— Look, it doesn't matter what I say. If you think that little of me, just come out and say it.'

Mark shook his head slowly. 'You don't get it, do you?' he asked, his voice flat. 'You just don't get it at all.'

'Apparently not.'

'What am I going to tell the boys when they get up in the morning?'

Caroline shrugged. 'The truth. That Mummy had to dash off for something very important, but she'll be back later tonight or the morning after.'

'You can't guarantee that.'

'Like I said, I'll make sure Dex knows he's running the show and I'll get the Super to draft in extra officers. You're right — it's my week off.'

'So why can't you do that over the phone?'

Caroline sighed. 'You'll just have to trust me that it's not that simple. If I'm there — even just for a few hours — I can see things for myself, and it'll make it clear to everyone that this is to be taken seriously. If I phone the Super and tell him I'm on holiday, and can he get someone else to do it, that won't wash. Anyway, an extra pair of hands for a day or so while they're bringing others in could literally be the difference between life and death.'

'So you'll be back Wednesday morning, absolute latest?'

'That's the plan.'

'Yeah, well we all know what happens with plans, don't we,' Mark said, more as a statement than a question.

'Here's your chance to trust me, then,' she replied, a part of her wishing she hadn't.

Mark took the car key out of his trouser pocket and held it out towards Caroline.

'I'll video call the kids in the morning,' she said. 'And I'm so sorry, Mark. I really am.'

Mark allowed her to kiss him on the cheek, then watched as she left.

15

'First of all, thanks for sticking around this late, guys,' Dexter said, addressing DCs Sara Henshaw and Aidan Chilcott. 'I know it's a bit weird me having to do this, especially when it's just the three of us, but — y'know. Procedure. So, I guess this is officially the first briefing on Operation Kayak, the investigation into the sudden deaths of Faith Pearson, Luke Grennan and Barbara Patchett. What's up, Aidan?' he added, turning to his grinning colleague.

'Operation Kayak,' Aidan replied. 'Up shit creek without a paddle. I know the computer names these things randomly, but it made me chuckle.'

Dexter smiled. 'Very good. But hopefully not an accurate description of our chances. On that note, I've had word from the boss that she's on her way back and will be in first thing tomorrow.'

'Isn't she meant to be on holiday?' Sara asked.

'You know what she's like,' Dexter replied. 'Besides which, we need all the help we can get. Okay, so, Faith's identity only became apparent to us within the last half an hour or so. Thankfully for us, she lived with a rather nervous and over-cautious flatmate, who called the police after Faith was an hour late back from her run. She sent over a couple of photos, which were clearly of the same girl who was found dead earlier tonight. Uniform visited the flat and were satisfied the body we have is Faith Pearson. We're in the process of locating her parents and family, in order to get an official ID on the body, but her Apple Watch paired immediately with her phone, which was seized, along with a tablet computer and a few other items which might help us piece things together.

'So at the moment we're looking at possible connections between three sudden and unexplained deaths. Two of them were pretty young — in their twenties — but Barbara was only in her early seventies, so hardly ready to meet her maker. All of them collapsed in a public place and died shortly after. None of them had any major health complications, except for high blood pressure in the case of Barbara, which was being successfully managed by medication. Luke and Faith were perfectly fit and healthy. Luke was a labourer, and Faith appears to have been a keen runner. I've spoken to the coroner and he's requested full Home

Office post-mortems, plus stomach contents and toxicology. Thankfully for us, he gets how quickly we need to move on this so he's asked for it to be fast-tracked. We can't speed up science, but we're hoping to have toxicology back before the end of the week. Without the full results, we don't have an official cause of death or any indication as to whether foul play was involved, but the sheer odds and circumstances mean I think it's safest if we assume it was. Without any physical signs of injury on any of our three victims, I expect we're looking at some form of poisoning.'

Sara raised her hand. 'Do you want me to do some research on possible candidates based on symptoms?'

Dexter considered this for a moment. 'It's not a bad idea,' he said, 'but we probably shouldn't prioritise it. Toxicology should be back before too long, and that'll confirm the presence and identity of any poison. We know Barbara and Luke seemed to display similar sorts of symptoms before they died — dizziness, nausea, generally seeming very off-colour. Barbara lost control of her bladder in the moments before she collapsed, which struck me as an anomaly. Faith, we don't know. She was already dead when she was found by a passer-by, so we don't know exactly how long she'd been there or what symptoms she had before she died. Our efforts are probably best spent on trying to identify patterns. Aidan, can you make it a priority to check CCTV in the surrounding area? We might be able to catch her somewhere. Then we can look at times, and work out when we know she was definitely alive. She was wearing a smart watch, so that should have kept a record of her heart rate and other vitals, especially if she was using it to track her run. We'll have accurate GPS, timings, everything we need to plot her movements earlier tonight, as well as being able to see what her body was doing.

'Sara, can you make a start on trying to identify any links these three people might have had? Social media connections, employment, family networks, weekend clubs, hobbies and pastimes, favourite Tellytubby — whatever. It could be something completely tenuous, but either way there'll be a link. There's something that means these specific three people died. We also need to get onto looking more carefully at any other recent deaths in the area that could be linked. If our three are connected, and if they were all killed by someone or something else, it's entirely possible Barbara wasn't the first. It's vital we determine that either way, especially if there's another victim who might hold the key to discovering that link between them all.'

Sara had been nodding while Dexter was talking, and occasionally typing into her computer. Dexter had assumed she was taking notes, but that now appeared not to be the case.

'Funny you should mention links,' she said, a smile growing across her face. 'I just put Luke Grennan and

Faith Pearson's names into Facebook, to see if there might be any crossover. Luke's profile's pretty much locked down, but Faith's is quite open. Her friends list is public. If you scroll down to the Ls, it looks like Luke is one of her Facebook friends.'

'They knew each other?' Dexter asked.

'Well, they certainly knew *of* each other,' Sara replied. 'We've all got people on Facebook who we met once at an event and promised to stay in touch with, or some random friend of a friend we vaguely remember from school. Either way, it looks like they were at least aware of each other and had some sort of prior connection.'

'They're similar sorts of ages, aren't they?' Aidan asked. 'Could be school.'

'Two years apart,' Dexter replied. 'Maybe one of them was in the same year as the other's sibling.'

'Entirely possible,' said Aidan. 'Oakham's not exactly a big place. It's not all that surprising that two people of a similar age would know each other.'

Dexter nodded slowly. 'True. But it's something, and at the moment it's all we've got. Keep digging. Find out what their connection is, if there's some sort of group or something they have in common. If there's anything that links to Barbara Patchett, even better. There won't be a huge amount more we can get done tonight, but lets put in those CCTV requests, do a bit of digital digging, then we can piece together anything we might need for speaking to families and friends tomorrow.'

He rubbed his eyes, already tired and tense, with the promise of further stresses lying ahead. He looked at his watch. It wouldn't be long until Caroline was back in Rutland, her calming presence ready to steer the ship. Tomorrow would be another day.

16

Caroline arrived at work early the next morning, feeling somewhere between holiday mode and the drag of her usual daily routine. Even though she'd got up early to head in, she was pleasantly surprised to see her team already hard at work, over-dedicated as always.

It was one of the things that made it harder to put the job second. Dexter, Sara and Aidan put her to shame with their work ethic as it was, and she was supposed to be the one leading the way and setting an example. It occurred to her that none of them had a marriage and children to maintain at the same time as the job, but she also knew they'd have little chance of the former while the latter ran the show.

'Morning,' she said as she walked in and made her way to her office, which, in practice, was a walled-off corner of the major incident room. She put her bag down, then stepped back into the main room. 'You guys are going to have to bring me up to speed pretty quickly. I'm due to have a word with the Super later this morning, so we can get some extra foot soldiers. Anything you can give me which might help my case would be much appreciated.'

'Do you think he'll go for that?' Aidan asked her.

'I've no idea. I hope so, because I'm still on holiday and I've got a husband on a beach in Suffolk somewhere, hopping mad and needing his car back. If we can make as much progress as possible today and get those extra hands to the pump, I'll be handing things back over to Dex for the rest of the week.'

Dexter clenched his jaw and smiled, trying not to show his discomfort. 'Alright. Well we'd better bring you up to speed, hadn't we?'

A couple of hours later, Caroline was poring over the sudden death reports completed by the officers at each respective scene, along with the information that had been given by the victims' families and witnesses, when there was a knock on her office door.

'Come in,' she said, not lifting her head.

'Boss,' Dexter said, his voice trembling with excitement. 'We've got something. You might want to come through.'

17

Caroline followed Dexter out of her office and into the main incident room, where Aidan was looking earnestly at his computer screen.

'Okay, so we were looking at the link between Faith Pearson and Luke Grennan, who we already knew were friends on Facebook,' Aidan said. 'I mentioned this to the digital guys who have Faith's smartwatch, phone and tablet, and they've found something really significant.'

'Alright,' Caroline said, wishing Aidan would get to the point. 'So what is it?'

'Facebook Messenger chats,' Aidan said, bringing up a document on his screen, which contained both screenshots of an online conversation. 'She didn't have her tablet locked down at all. No PIN, nothing. Her

Facebook account was already logged in, so they were able to access her messages.'

Caroline leaned in closer and read the words on the screen.

The name at the top of the chat window stood out immediately. *Luke Grennan.* Underneath it, a conversation played out — Luke's messages on the left, alongside a small thumbnail image of his profile picture, with Faith's messages on the right.

Hey you. Long time!

Haha, yeah it's been a while! How you been? x

Yeah all good here thanks. Just busy with work and stuff. Saw your post - you not with Andy any more? x

Nooooo we split up months ago! Less said about that the better 😂 x

Noted!! 😂😂 Men eh??

Would be good to go for a drink and catch up some time if your up for it?? x

Yeah that'd be good actually! x

Maybe re live some old times too!! xx

Woah slow down cowboy 😂 Aren't you engaged?! x

Didn't mean that!! 😂😂 Just meant in general!! x

😂😂 Soz - already had a couple trying it on already! Drinks & general sounds good to me x

Some lads have no shame 😂😂 You got what's app? x

Yep - 07700918172 x

Cool will add u now xx

'Is that it?' Caroline asked.

'Yeah, it ends there. Looks like they moved the conversation straight onto WhatsApp.'

'Alright. Are we able to access her WhatsApp messages?'

'Not yet. She didn't have it installed on her tablet, and her phone's locked with a six-digit PIN. We're working on getting access to that. Luke's only got a phone, but that's locked down too. Hopefully we'll be able to get in soon. That Facebook conversation's from two weeks ago, so we've potentially got a fortnight's worth of WhatsApp chats to go through. Could be plenty of evidential material in there.'

'Fingers crossed,' Caroline replied.

'Is it just me, or does it sound like they had a bit of history?' Dexter asked.

Caroline nodded. 'I thought that. They clearly knew each other. Especially those mentions of old times.'

'It's the "slow down cowboy" bit that jumps out at me,' Aidan said. 'Straight after Luke mentions "old times". Then Faith asks him if he's engaged. Sounds to me like they had some history there. She seems to straightaway assume he's talking about sex, or some sort of intimate relationship.'

Caroline nodded again. 'He knew that, too. Immediately says he didn't mean it like that. They're obviously both really aware of some sort of shared past. Excellent stuff, Aidan. Really good work. I think we need to prioritise speaking to Luke's fiancée, as well as this Andy chap. Faith's ex, by the look of things. Doesn't sound like she was keen on talking about him, so there's a possibility he might've found out Luke and Faith had been seeing more of each other, which would be a reasonable motive to do something about it — especially if he's an unhinged sort of person. We need to identify this Andy, find out who he is and speak to him. Remember, this is purely to find out more about Faith and Luke. As far as any family or friends are concerned, this is not a murder inquiry. We have to wait for post-mortem results first. We can't go causing distress to the families until we've got good reason to believe their loved ones were killed by anything other than Mother Nature.'

'I've had a look on Faith's friends list again,' Sara said, squinting at her computer. 'No Andys or Andrews on there.'

'None at all?' Caroline asked.

'Nope. She's only got ninety-six friends listed, though, so probably not beyond the realms of statistical probability.'

'The flatmate should know. If not, her family will at least have a surname for him, or we'll be able to find WhatsApp messages stored in her phone's history. Let's get everything combed through, see if we can put a surname on this Andy character.' Caroline looked at her watch, and gave an involuntary swallow. 'Right. On that note, I've got to dash. Got that meeting with the Super. Wish me luck.'

18

Caroline stepped into Chief Superintendent Derek Arnold's office and waited for him to tell her to be seated. Although the structure of Rutland Police was unconventional in many ways, there were certain conventions that Caroline couldn't let go. Respect for her superiors was one of them.

'How was the holiday?' Arnold asked, in a perfect example of the force's unorthodox setup. When she'd been in the Met, she was pretty sure she'd never even *seen* officers who were three ranks senior; she'd certainly never encountered one who'd been familiar with her family holidays.

'It was lovely, thanks. Although shorter than we'd anticipated.'

'Oh?'

Caroline took a deep breath and began to speak.

'We've had three suspicious and unexpected deaths in Oakham since Sunday. All healthy people who dropped dead after feeling a bit ill for a short while before. Two of them were young adults, one was a woman in her seventies. Completely out of the blue, all of them. We're hoping to get more soon, but we've already discovered the two youngest victims knew each other. We've still got information coming to light, but it looks like they might have been romantically or sexually involved in the past, and they recently got back in contact with each other again.'

'Victims?' Arnold asked, an eyebrow raised. 'Is this a murder investigation?'

'Yes and no,' Caroline replied. 'We've opened a case, but until we get the post-mortem results we're playing our cards close to our chest, especially when it comes to family and friends.'

'Very wise. Well, do keep me posted.'

'Yes, sir. In fact, DS Antoine will probably be the point of contact. He's leading the investigation.'

Arnold cocked his head slightly. 'Oh?'

'I'm still on leave. I'm not due back until next Monday. Actually, that's sort of what I wanted to speak to you about. I was hoping we might be able to get another couple of bodies in. It's such a fast-moving case already, and for all we know there could be others who are linked. There's no way the team would be able to cope with just the three of them. Especially if we end up with more victims.'

'If they are victims, of course.'

'Of course. But I think it's best that we assume the worst, if that makes sense.'

Arnold steepled his hands and nodded slowly. 'Sensible, yes. You do know if you're recalled from annual leave you'll get time and a half back, plus double time for the first two days. You'd be able to lead the case and come out of it with a longer break than you had in the first place.'

'I understand that, sir, but it's not quite that simple. My family are already there. We've been staying on the Suffolk coast. I actually got back in the early hours of this morning, after DS Antoine called to tell me about the third death. I only came back for the day to steady the ship and speak to you about reinforcements.'

Caroline was sure the chief superintendent's eyebrows gave the slightest of flutters, which she read as him being less than impressed with her approach. In the Met, it would have been a no-brainer. Annual leave was annual leave, and there were always more than enough officers floating around who could be drafted in. Any major investigation would have dozens, if not more, detectives working across it, as well as a host of other teams. Here, though, things were very different. The concept of a Detective Inspector going back to her family holiday just as a potential murder case was opening was completely alien in this neck of the woods.

'I see,' Arnold said, his voice level. 'So, in your opinion, this is serious enough to warrant drafting in extra officers from elsewhere, but not quite serious enough to lose a couple of days of holiday over.'

'That's not quite what I—'

'This is precisely what EMSOU's for, Caroline.'

Caroline clenched her jaw and hoped Arnold hadn't noticed. He was right. The East Midlands Special Operations Unit was designed to handle major inquiries on behalf of all police forces in the East Midlands area — all of which were far bigger and better resourced than Rutland. She'd already had to fight tooth and nail over the past couple of years to be allowed to keep hold of cases, and there was no way she was going to roll back on that commitment now.

'I know,' she replied, looking straight into Arnold's eyes. 'But I've got results every single time, without needing anything from them. I don't intend for that to change now. DS Antoine's more than capable of leading the investigation. And anyway, it's entirely possible I wouldn't make a huge amount of difference on my own. If this case becomes as complex as I think it might, we're going to need significantly more manpower than that.'

Arnold sighed. 'It's not quite as easy as rustling up some spare officers, you know. There are all sorts of hoops to jump through, and with budgetary constraints as they are, there's no hope of anything while we're not even certain there *is* a case. When are we expecting post mortem results?'

'I'm not sure,' Caroline replied. 'Hopefully later today or tomorrow morning.'

'Are you sticking around in the meantime?'

'To be honest, that all depends on how long they take. Please don't repeat this to anyone, but things have been a bit wobbly at home over the past few months. The holiday was meant to be time spent together as a family, away from the pressures of work. I took a huge risk even coming back in the first place.'

Arnold looked at her for a few moments, then nodded. 'Okay. Look, I'll put some feelers out. I can't do much more than that until we can at least confirm these are murders we're investigating, and I'll need much more detail on what's needed in terms of resources. You spearhead that, so DS Antoine can focus solely on leading the investigation. He's got you to lean on if needed. If we get everything prepared upfront, then if the post mortem results come back and we're definitely looking at a murder investigation, we can press the button immediately. Can you stick around until then?'

Caroline steeled herself. Although the coroner had put pressure on the pathologists to fast-track the post-mortems, there was no knowing if this would actually happen. She thought of Mark, and the promise she gave him that she'd be back first thing in the morning, if not later that evening. Would the results be in by then? It was possible. Likely, even. But certainly far from guaranteed. She knew she should call him and let him know she might be back later than expected, but was it worth putting that cat amongst the pigeons before a delay was certain?

'Yes, of course,' she said. 'I'll be here.'

19

Caroline left Derek Arnold's office feeling both energised and deflated in equal measure. Now it was a waiting game, and not one she relished.

She'd decided to go and see Luke Grennan's fiancée herself, as well as Faith Pearson's flatmate. She'd called both before leaving the office, to make sure they'd be in. She'd never been keen on desk work, and the mind-numbing nature of that would cause her stress levels to rise even more. Besides which, nothing came close to being able to look into the whites of people's eyes.

She knew she was going to have to tread carefully. As far as their families and friends were concerned, Barbara Patchett, Luke Grennan and Faith Pearson had all died suddenly and tragically, but not suspiciously. To have the police sniffing around and asking questions

could raise more than a few eyebrows at best, or —
worse — cause great distress.

'How much longer?' Mark asked, his voice coming
through her car's speakers.

'Only a few hours at most. We could still get the
post-mortem results today, but if it rolls over into
tomorrow I might not be able to get back until the
afternoon or evening.'

'Evening?' Mark said, the frustration clear in his
voice.

'At worst. But that might not even happen. I'm only
telling you as a worst case scenario, just in case.'

'Come off it, Caz. You're only telling me that
because it's practically a dead cert, same as you always
do. I'd rather you just told me you'd be back later and
actually arrived earlier. Then I wouldn't always feel so
let down.'

Caroline sighed quietly. 'Honestly, Mark. I'm not. I
promise you, I'm only letting you know the worst case
scenario. It's nowhere near a dead cert. In fact, the
whole reason I'm calling you now is because I *didn't*
want to over-promise and under-deliver. This is actually
me trying to be as honest and upfront as possible.'

Mark was silent for a moment. 'Look, I'm going to
go. I've got to sort the kids out.'

'Mark…'

The three bleeps through the car's speakers told her
that her husband had already ended the call.

A few moments later, Caroline parked up outside the small terraced house Luke had shared with his fiancée, Sophie Pendleton. Caroline knocked on the door, and a few seconds later a man in his sixties opened it.

'Hi, come in,' he said, having clearly been expecting her. 'I'm Grant, Sophie's dad.'

Although Caroline had never met Grant Pendleton before, she imagined he hadn't looked quite so ashen and beaten before today. Without him having said a word, she could already tell he'd been fond of his future son-in-law, and was grieving the family loss as much as anybody.

Caroline made her way through to the living room, where she found Sophie half-sitting, half-lying on the sofa, being cradled by her mother.

'This is my wife, Pam,' Grant said. 'Sophie, it's the police.'

'Hi Sophie. My name's Caroline,' she said, deliberately opting not to provide her rank. She wouldn't lie if asked, but she reasoned in the meantime there was no harm in them assuming she was some form of back-office staff. In many ways, they'd be correct. 'First of all, can I say how sorry I am for your loss. I can't even begin to imagine what you're going through right now, and I'm really sorry to intrude at such a time.'

Sophie nodded gently, her eyes closed.

'We understand,' her father said. 'Especially if it helps us find out what happened. It just seems so... sudden. You can't quite get your head around it, you know? It doesn't seem real somehow.'

'It can take a while to sink in,' Caroline offered. 'Especially when it's been so unexpected. But, as you say, my job is to help find out what happened to Luke. I'm confident we can do that. Are you going to be okay for me to ask you a few questions, Sophie? Nothing too taxing, I promise.'

Sophie nodded again.

'Should we stay, or...?' Pam asked, leaving the question open.

'Entirely up to you, but it might be better for me and Sophie to speak one-to-one, if she'd be comfortable with that.'

Caroline looked again at Sophie, who shrugged slightly. 'It's fine, Mum. I'll shout if I need you.'

Caroline watched as Grant and Pam left the room and went upstairs — the only place in the tiny house they'd have any chance of getting out of earshot.

'Sorry,' she said to Sophie once they'd gone. 'You'd be amazed at the things people don't like saying in front of others sometimes. These things are so much easier and far more successful if we're able to get all the facts.'

'It's cool,' Sophie said, her voice almost a whisper, hoarse through hours of crying.

Caroline took a deep breath then slowly exhaled. 'I

understand you and Luke were planning to marry, is that right?'

Sophie nodded slowly, her eyes brimming with tears again. 'Yeah. Yeah, we were.' She offered no more information, but Caroline didn't need any at that moment. The grief on her face told her everything she needed to know.

'Had he mentioned feeling unwell at all? Either earlier that day, or even any recent illnesses?'

'No, nothing. He's always been really healthy. He had a cold at Christmas, but that was about it. That's the thing I can't understand. It's just so… I don't know what to say.'

'Was he on any medication at all? Supplements, even?'

'Only for his anxiety. I don't think he took them all the time, though. Just every now and then when he needed to.'

This surprised Caroline. It was the first she'd heard of it. 'What was it called, do you know?'

'Propranolol, I think it is. It just slows his heart and stops him shaking and sweating and things if he has a panic attack coming on.'

Caroline jotted this down in her notebook. 'Okay. Would he have taken it yesterday morning, do you think?'

'Probably. Work made him anxious, especially on a Monday morning or after a few days off. I don't know for sure, but yeah, I imagine he would've done.'

'And what if he didn't? Might that have caused the sort of symptoms he had?'

Sophie seemed to ponder this for a moment. 'I don't know. I mean, kind of. It'd mean his heart would race more if he got anxious, but it wouldn't be enough to… you know. It's not a lifesaving medicine or anything. The worst he'd get without it would be a panic attack.'

Far from pleasant and ideal, but not typically a life-threatening situation, Caroline thought.

'It's good to see you taking an interest,' Caroline said. 'Sorry, I hope that didn't sound weird. You'd be surprised how many people don't even know what their partner's medication is for. You obviously knew each other very well.'

A faint flash of a smile crossed Sophie's face. 'Yeah. Yeah, we did.'

'How long were you together?'

'Just over three years,' Sophie said, her voice leaden with bittersweet memories.

'A long time. Was it your first serious relationship?'

'It was mine, but not Luke's.'

Caroline cocked her head a little. 'Oh?'

'He was with a girl for a couple of years before we met. Faith.'

Caroline was thankful Sophie wasn't looking directly at her, because she would have struggled to hide her reaction. She was pleased Sophie had offered up the information without her having to probe and raise suspicion. The revelation Luke and Faith had been in a serious relationship prior to his meeting Sophie was huge. But the overriding thought in Caroline's mind at that moment was that she might have to have to show her cards earlier than planned.

'Ah,' she said, trying to sound only casually interested. 'Was that a source of anxiety for him, or did they keep in touch?'

'She went off with another guy,' Sophie said. 'So no, they definitely didn't keep in touch.'

There was very little point in asking Sophie if she knew about the Facebook and WhatsApp messages, Caroline realised. Not right now, anyway. If Sophie believed Luke and Faith hadn't spoken for some time, there was no benefit in mentioning the messages. She didn't want to cause undue stress, and in any case she figured it would be a better idea to speak to Faith's flatmate first. If Luke'd had dishonourable intentions in contacting Faith, it was to be expected that he hadn't told his fiancée. However, it was just the sort of thing a woman might mention to her flatmate. Caroline made a mental note.

'And how did he get on with work?' she asked. 'You mentioned it made him anxious. Do you know why?'

Sophie's face changed slightly, from grief and shock to an empathetic sadness.

'I think it was mostly the people he worked with,' she said, attracting Caroline's attention.

'How do you mean?'

Sophie let out a sad, wistful sigh. 'Luke's a complicated person,' she said, her voice beginning to crack. 'He had a difficult childhood. He was such a smart guy, so clever in so many ways, but he just didn't do well at school. He wasn't really built for it, I guess, and being dyslexic didn't help. He never really went into any details, but I get the impression he had some trouble at school. Bullying, that sort of thing. I think it all just made him an anxious person in general. He never really liked pranks and banter and all of that stuff. He was quiet. Gentle. Not the sort of person you'd expect to do well on building sites, if you see what I mean.'

'I think so,' Caroline said, smiling. 'He sounds like a lovely guy.'

Sophie clamped her lips together and nodded gently, tears filling her eyes.

'Was there anyone in particular he'd fallen out with? At work, I mean.'

Sophie shook her head. 'No. I don't think so. He wasn't the sort of person to fall out with people. He didn't do conflict, didn't fight. Didn't even do arguments most of the time, unless it was something he was really passionate about. He just preferred to keep the peace and get on with life.'

Caroline watched Sophie's face as she registered the irony of those last few words.

'Sorry,' she said. 'I hope I'm not upsetting you by asking you these questions. It's just that while we don't know how Luke died, we have to keep every possibility open.'

'I understand,' Sophie replied. 'It's okay, I know you're just doing your job. But honestly, in all the time I knew Luke I don't think I ever heard him raise his voice. I know you never met him, but he really was the loveliest, gentlest person. No-one would've wanted to harm him.'

Although she'd been caught out once or twice in the past, Caroline tended to be pretty good at spotting when people were being honest with her. And even if what Sophie was telling her wasn't the whole truth, it was almost certainly *her* truth, as far as she was aware.

In Caroline's mind, she was already starting to think about the questions she'd ask Faith's flatmate.

20

Caroline closed her car door and sat in silence for a few moments. Although she'd met many families who'd been touched by tragedy, there were always some that lived long in the memory. She had a feeling Sophie and Luke would do so too. A young couple in their prime, making their wedding arrangements and planning the rest of their lives together, snatched from them in the most sudden and unexpected way.

She'd often heard people say how cruel it was to see a loved one die of a long illness, and that was something she'd never understood. Of course it was cruel. It was horrendous. But it gave you one advantage over the alternative: time to prepare. Sophie hadn't had that. She'd watched her future husband leave for work in the morning, looking forward to seeing him again at teatime, where they'd no doubt talk more about their plans for the future. He'd never come home, and she'd never got the chance to say goodbye.

There would have been so many things she would have wanted to say to him, if only she'd known. If only she'd had time to prepare. She'd never have been ready — no-one was — but there was comfort to be had in the knowledge that nothing needed to be left unsaid. If you couldn't choose when to go, Caroline thought the best alternative was to at least know it was coming.

She'd had her own experiences, of course. Although she'd been told a few months earlier that her cancer treatment had been successful, she knew there was always the chance it would come back. And even if it didn't, she still had the knowledge of how it felt to see her own death on the horizon. She'd never been told she would die, of course. It had always been serious, but treatable. But whereas death had never been a consideration or possibility at any point in her life before that, it had suddenly taken on a very real identity.

She started her car and began the journey to Faith Pearson's former home, where her flatmate, Aimee Clifford-Parks, would be waiting for her. She was barely a minute into her journey when her phone rang. Pressing a button on her steering wheel, she answered the call on the car's bluetooth system.

'Caroline Hills.'

'Boss, it's me,' Dexter said. 'We've got post-mortem results back for Barbara Patchett.'

'Alright, good. Anything interesting?'

'Not really. Acute pulmonary oedema and a heart attack due to severe coronary with cardiac tamponade.'

'Excellently read, Dex. Now tell me what it means.'

'I asked them that too. In short, she had a heart attack caused by fluid building up around the heart. That meant it couldn't deal with the blood supply to her lungs, so more fluid built up in the tissue.'

'I see,' Caroline replied. 'It doesn't sound all that suspicious, though, does it?'

Dexter paused for a moment before speaking. 'Not on the face of it. But we're expecting toxicology results to follow, so we should have a better idea then.'

'You thinking poisoning?'

'That's my hunch,' Dexter replied. 'I'd much rather I was wrong and that it's all a huge coincidence, but that's probably wishful thinking.'

Caroline murmured her agreement. 'If it's any help, I just spoke to Sophie Pendleton, Luke Grennan's fiancée. She said Luke and Faith were together for a couple of years. Sounds like it was pretty serious. She was under the impression they hadn't been in touch recently, though. I didn't tell her otherwise.'

'Probably for the best. I think our focus needs to be on finding Faith's other ex. This Andy guy. It seems a little convenient that Luke and Faith get back in touch with each other, and within a couple of weeks they're both dead. If we can identify him, we might be onto something.'

'Agreed,' Caroline said. 'Still doesn't explain Barbara Patchett, though. What's her connection to all this?'

'I don't know. Maybe finding this Andy will give us answers to that. What if the victims aren't all linked to each other, but to the killer?'

'Maybe she was caught in the crossfire, so to speak. Focusing on her could be a complete red herring.'

'It's possible. But how do you accidentally poison someone you don't even know?'

Caroline had to admit he had a point. 'What about stomach contents?' she asked. 'Anything unusual?'

'Apparently not,' Dexter replied. 'Looks like she'd had a pretty standard breakfast. A couple of croissants, a cup of coffee and some grapefruit juice. Obviously more of a continental girl than a full English. I honestly don't know what's wrong with people.'

'Remind me not to invite you round for breakfast,' Caroline said, smiling. 'Although I think Barbara and I would've got on pretty well.'

'I dunno. Dangerous things, these croissants. And here's proof if ever it was needed.'

Caroline tried her best not to laugh and encourage

him. 'I tell you what, Dex. Why don't you get off the phone and make yourself more useful. I'm on my way to speak to Aimee Clifford-Parks, Faith's flatmate. With any luck, we'll have an identity for this Andy before too long.'

A couple of minutes after the call had ended, Caroline parked up in a visitors' space outside the block of flats where Faith had lived. She got out of her car, approached the building and pressed the buzzer for the flat.

'Hello?' came the voice at the other end of the intercom.

'Aimee Clifford-Parks? It's Caroline Hills from Rutland Police. We spoke on the phone.'

'Sure. Come up,' Aimee said, followed by a buzzing sound that indicated the door was now unlocked.

Caroline made her way up to the flat, arriving just as Aimee opened the door.

'Aimee, hi,' she said, stepping inside. 'I'm really sorry to hear about Faith. I know it must be a difficult time for you.'

'Yeah. It's such a shock,' Aimee replied, clearly a woman of few words.

'I like what you've done with the flat,' Caroline said, admiring the decor. 'Very modern. Tasteful.'

'Thanks.'

Realising an invitation wasn't going to be forthcoming, Caroline sat down on one of two sofas, spreading her notebook open on her lap.

'So, how long did you and Faith live together?' she asked.

'Only about six months. Not long.'

'How did you meet?'

'I answered an ad. For the flat.'

'Oh, so you didn't know each other before that?'

'No. A friend of mine shared a post she'd put online. She was looking for a flatmate, I was looking for a flat. Rest's history, really.'

'Do you know why she was looking for a new flatmate?' Caroline asked, by now having picked up that Aimee responded far better to direct questions than fluffing round the edges and avoiding getting to the point.

'A relationship break-up. She didn't really talk much about it.'

Caroline made a show of noting this down, as if she hadn't already put two and two together.

'Do you know anything about the relationship? His name, where he lives now, anything like that?' she asked, before registering the look on Aimee's face. 'Just for background, I mean. We like to build up a full picture. Besides which, there might be people we need to inform.'

Aimee shuffled uncomfortably. 'I'm not sure Faith would've wanted you informing him, if I'm honest. She barely mentioned him, but when she did she made it pretty clear they didn't get on anymore. Nasty breakup, from what I could gather.'

'I see,' Caroline said, giving a smile. 'But it still helps to build up a picture. Was his name Luke?' she asked, knowing it wasn't, but wondering if it might prompt something.

'No, some guy called Alan or Adam or something.'

'Andy?'

This seemed to cause a flicker of recognition in Aimee. 'Might be,' she said. 'I think they'd been together a while.'

Caroline tried to piece together the information in her head. As she understood it, Faith and Luke had been going out up until a couple of years ago, when Faith had left him for Andy. Then, it seems, Andy and Faith had moved in together, until they split up, leaving Faith without a flatmate. Enter Aimee.

'What sort of impression did you get about him?' Caroline asked. 'Nice enough guy, or maybe something else?'

Aimee shrugged. 'Nothing really. I never met him. Wouldn't know him if I walked past him in the street. Faith never said a good word about him, but then she wouldn't, would she? If they'd just broken up, I mean.'

'I don't know. It can happen amicably.'

'Not this time, from what I could gather.'

'You don't happen to know his surname, do you?'

'No idea. Sorry. Why do you ask?'

'Just building a picture,' Caroline replied, smiling. 'I understand it was you who reported Faith missing. Is that right?'

'Yeah. She went out for her run, and said she'd be half an hour or so. Then when she didn't come back, I panicked.'

Caroline looked at Aimee. This wasn't a woman who seemed prone to panicking. If anything, she was remarkably calm under the circumstances.

'That's okay,' she said. 'We all panic sometimes. To be honest, it's a good thing you did. Otherwise no-one would've known she was missing, and it would've taken longer to identify her.'

'You would've got there eventually,' Aimee replied.

An odd comment, Caroline thought, before asking, 'Do you often panic about things? You seem very calm to me.'

'If I seem weird it's because I'm autistic.'

Caroline blinked a few times. 'Okay. I definitely wouldn't say weird.'

'Most people would,' Aimee replied. 'No-one ever really knows how to read me. Which is fine, because I don't know how to read them either.'

Aimee gave a smile, silently inviting Caroline to

enjoy her joke with her. Caroline supposed it was one she'd told many times before.

'Does it have much of an impact on your life?'

'Yes and no. Sometimes people think I'm being rude or off with them. Either that or I get confused about boundaries and come across as clingy. Most of the time I just get on with it and keep myself to myself.'

'Not really a people person?' Caroline asked, smiling.

'Not really, no.'

'You and me both. How did Faith seem before she left for her run?'

Aimee thought about this for a moment. 'Fine, I think. She didn't really say much. She got home from work and was rushing about sorting bits out. I was watching Netflix. It's not like we were best friends or anything. She just couldn't afford to keep the flat by herself and I was looking for a place to live, so we sort of paired up. We didn't really socialise or go out together or anything.'

'Did she seem okay physically? Was she ill or unwell at all?'

Aimee shook her head. 'Not that she mentioned. I know she'd been complaining about getting fat recently, so she wanted to start running again. I think she busted her leg a little while ago.'

'Had she been back running long?' Caroline asked.

'No, this was her first time in ages. I did tell her to

take it easy. Do you think she had one of those undiagnosed heart problems? Lots of footballers have them. You hear about them keeling over on the pitch. My cousin does St John's Ambulance, and he was telling me that happened at a game he was at. Good job they were there, or the guy would've died.'

Caroline took a moment to re-centre herself. In a matter of minutes, Aimee had gone from one-word answers to vaguely irrelevant rambles. She supposed this meant she was comfortable talking to her, which could be an advantage.

'Maybe,' she said. 'We don't actually know what the cause of death was just yet, but we're hoping to find out soon, once the post-mortem results come back.'

'I saw a programme about that once,' Aimee replied, pulling a face that looked like she'd just sniffed a bin. 'I don't know how anybody can do that job. I mean, it's really fascinating in one way, but if you think about it, you're basically just cutting people up.'

'I think there's a little more to it than that, but I see your point. On the plus side, at least it'll give us some answers, and we can find out what happened to Faith.'

As Caroline spoke, a thought occurred to her. If Faith had been living with the elusive Andy, his name would've been on the papers for the flat.

'Sorry, unrelated question, but is the flat rented or owned?'

Aimee cocked her head slightly. 'Well, technically both.'

'How do you mean?'

'Faith and I rent it, but obviously it's owned by the landlord. We just pay to be able to live here. So technically it's owned *and* rented.'

Caroline smiled. 'I understand. And are you listed on the papers?'

Aimee's face fell. 'No. I'm not. I just used to pay my portion of the rent to Aimee, and she paid the landlord. I didn't sign any paperwork or anything. Does that mean I'm going to get into trouble?'

'Not with me, you're not. I'm not really in the business of worrying about sub-letting. Do you know who the landlord is?' Caroline asked, more avenues now opening up in her mind.

If Aimee wasn't listed as an official tenant, there was a chance Andy wouldn't have been either. Caroline had hoped she could find his full name that way, but that was now looking less likely. And why would Faith need to sub-let? It seemed more likely that Faith owned the flat, and that both Andy and, subsequently, Aimee, had been staying there and paying their way. She made a note to check the deeds with the Land Registry.

'I don't know the owner's name, no,' Aimee replied. 'Is that a problem?'

'Not really. It'd just speed things up a bit. We can find out either way.'

'Actually,' Aimee said, leaning forward conspiratorially, 'there is something I might know.'

'Go on.'

'Now, this might sound like a conspiracy theory to you, but I've been reading a few blogs recently.'

Caroline pursed her lips and tried to force a smile. She had a feeling this was going to be a long day.

21

Caroline stepped out of her car and checked her watch, wondering what Mark and the boys were doing right now. Josh and Archie would be enjoying themselves regardless, but Mark would no doubt be sitting with a black cloud over him, angry and frustrated at her for not being able to be in two places at once.

She silently berated herself for thinking this way. It wasn't as if it was his fault she'd disappeared halfway through their holiday. If she was honest with herself, she did feel angry that he seemed not to understand the seriousness of her job, but she couldn't blame him for that. She knew she was projecting. It wasn't Mark who failed to understand. It was her. She hadn't appreciated the damage she'd done to her family over the years. Truthfully, she wasn't sure she fully understood it even now.

Once, Mark had called her a workaholic. Just the once. Her reaction had been enough to make sure he didn't repeat it. If she thought about it, though, he was right. In many ways, it was an addiction. Over the years, she'd seen plenty of interviews and documentaries with gambling addicts, and she'd been struck by the ways in which they described their addiction. It wasn't that they didn't know what damage they were causing. It wasn't that they didn't hear the pleas of their loved ones. It was the sheer strength of compulsion, the push to nail that one last big win. And, in many ways, it was a form of self-harm. It didn't matter whether they knew the damage they were doing to themselves. If anything, they reasoned they deserved it as a form of punishment. But did she really feel that she *deserved* Mark to leave her? It was an interesting word.

The problem was, they were both as stubborn as each other. At any other time, she'd be the last person to make first contact after someone had hung up on her, but she wasn't going to give up on doing the right thing.

Still standing in the car park outside Oakham Police Station, she took her phone out of her pocket and opened WhatsApp before she had a chance to think twice. She tapped Mark's name, typed out a quick message to him, then sent it.

Feeling the warmth of the sun on the back of her neck, she made her way through the front door and headed for the incident room.

'Good timing,' Aidan said as she closed the door behind her. 'Looks like we might've made a breakthrough.'

'Go on,' Caroline replied, walking over to him.

'Okay, so this might provide more questions than answers, but we've had the preliminary post-mortem results back on Luke Grennan. The cause is still inconclusive, mainly because of his age and health. Something didn't quite sit right with them. Like with Barbara Patchett, there's fluid in the pericardial sac and also in parts of the lungs. I didn't really understand most of it, but they're sending over the full details. Here's where it gets interesting, though. Not only were there concerns over the true cause of death, but they did an analysis of Luke's stomach contents, too, and noted what he'd eaten that morning. Toast, tea and grapefruit juice.'

Caroline paused for a moment. 'And what did Barbara Patchett have on Sunday?'

'Croissants, coffee and grapefruit juice,' Aidan replied.

'Grapefruit juice. They both drank grapefruit juice.'

'Either that or the milk was off,' Dexter quipped.

'Barbara Patchett had her coffee black,' Aidan said.

'Alright. I wasn't being serious.'

'Do we know where this grapefruit juice came from?' Caroline asked. 'Do we have a brand? The shop it was bought from?'

Aidan shook his head. 'Not yet. We only heard a moment or two before you came back. I'm literally about to call Brian Patchett and Sophie Pendleton now.'

'Alright. Good. Call Aimee Clifford-Parks, too. She'll have either never heard of grapefruit juice, or she'll have memorised the entire set of nutritional information and the barcode number.'

'Take your word for it,' Dexter said. 'If you call her, that'll speed things up. Aidan, can you get onto Brian Patchett please?'

'And leave you phoning up the distressed and newly-single woman, you mean?'

Dexter put his hand to his chest in mock offence. 'Please. A bereaved woman who's just lost the love of her life, you mean. It wouldn't seem fair subjecting her to a call from you. Not after everything she's been through.'

'Shall we pack it in and crack on, then?' Caroline said, trying to inject some professionalism into proceedings. 'I'll call Aimee Clifford-Parks now. I'll either be out in thirty seconds, or someone'll have to come and rescue me.'

Caroline headed into her office and sat down at her desk. Once she'd looked up Aimee's mobile number, she picked up the phone and dialled.

'Hypertrophic cardiomyopathy,' Aimee said, answering the call.

'Sorry? Hello, it's Caroline Hills, from Rutland Police. I was at your flat a little while ago.'

'Yes, I know. I saved your number in my phone. Hypertrophic cardiomyopathy. The heart condition those athletes had and didn't even know about. I remembered in the end. HCM, they sometimes call it. Was that what killed Faith?'

Caroline took a moment to realign herself. 'We don't think so, no,' she said eventually.

'It's just you said you'd ring when you had some news, so I thought maybe that's what you were ringing for.'

'Actually, I was wondering if you might be able to help.'

'Ooh, very Father Brown.'

'It's not quite that exciting, unfortunately. I need you to check something for me.'

'Okay, shoot.'

Caroline had visions of Aimee sitting keenly at the other end of the phone with a notepad and pen.

'This might sound a bit odd, but do you know if Faith drank grapefruit juice?'

Aimee was silent for a few moments. 'Grapefruit juice. Grapefruit juice…' she murmured to herself. 'I don't think we have any of that. Hold on, I'm looking in the fridge… No. No grapefruit juice.'

'Might she have brought some home from work?

Was there a shop she used to grab a drink from before her runs, maybe?'

'Oh. That's a point. She came home with a few things she'd picked up after work. Maybe she bought it there?'

'Maybe, yes. Do you know which shop?'

'Yeah, the bag's on the table. It's a convenience store in Melton. Hold on, I'll send you a photo.'

Caroline's instinct was to ask her to simply read out the name of the shop, but she realised it was probably easier to run with it. 'Lovely, thanks,' she said, her phone buzzing a moment or two later as the picture arrived. 'And there's definitely no grapefruit juice in the bag?'

'No, definitely not. There's some organic oat biscuits, a bag of fair-trade mixed nuts and a packet of beetroot crisps. She's on a health kick.'

'How about the bin?'

'What about it?'

'Is there an empty bottle in there?' Caroline asked, trying not to sound frustrated.

'That's a point. I didn't think of that. Hold on, I'll have a look.'

Caroline listened as Aimee poked at the contents of the bin.

'Ah-ha, here we go. "Organic grapefruit juice." What does that even mean? Who's ever seen a man-made grapefruit? I mean, there are those plastic ones in kids' toy sets, but you're not going to try and squeeze juice out of one of those, are you?'

'What's the brand name on the carton?'

'It's a bottle.'

Caroline paused for the briefest of moments to stop herself from snapping. 'Okay, what's the brand name on the bottle?'

'Squeeze The Day.'

As she wrote the name down in her notepad in front of her, Caroline felt the slightest bit of tension beginning to ease.

22

The team were back in the office early that Wednesday morning, in full expectation that Faith Pearson's post-mortem results would be back. Before long, their prayers were answered and Caroline had assembled everyone for a briefing.

'I'll cut straight to the important bits,' she said, keen not to waste a single moment. 'The report shows that Faith ultimately died from the same cardiac symptoms as Barbara Patchett and Luke Grennan. All in all, it's looking eerily familiar. We're still waiting on toxicology results of course, and won't get those until tomorrow at the earliest, but an examination of Faith's stomach contents revealed the presence of grapefruit juice. So I'd say that's looking very much like our missing link.'

'It pretty much confirms poisoning or contamination, then,' Dexter said. 'And we've got a brand name for the juice, which gives us a strong starting point.'

'It does, but we have to tread carefully,' Caroline replied. 'I've organised a meeting with the comms team to discuss potential messaging and public safety warnings. If we're seriously considering the possibility that Squeeze The Day's juice has been contaminated or poisoned, the ramifications could be huge. There's a real balancing act between ensuring public safety and being left wide open to legal action if we're wrong. Dex?'

'Sara was asking the other day about whether she should start researching possible poisons or substances that might cause those symptoms. I wondered whether that might be a good idea now we're more certain about the poisoning aspect.'

Caroline nodded. 'It certainly wouldn't hurt. We'll know either tomorrow or Friday when toxicology comes back, but there's no harm getting ahead of the game, especially if we're going to have to pay a visit to Squeeze The Day. Forewarned is forearmed, and all that.'

There was a knock at the door, and a uniformed officer peered in.

'Mike Farrington here to see you, ma'am.'

'Lovely, thank you. Come on, Dex. We've got quite a day ahead of us.'

23

Caroline sat down in the meeting room with Dexter and Mike Farrington, the force's Head of Corporate Communications and Engagement. Although the title sounded over-elaborate and unwarranted, Mike's job was crucial when it came to engaging with the public and outside bodies.

Recent developments meant public engagement and communications would be crucial, especially if others were likely to be at risk. Although minimising harm was the key aim, they couldn't risk causing unnecessary trauma or damaging innocently connected businesses or parties.

'Okay, I think we're going to need to tread carefully on this,' Caroline said, knowing they needed to make progress as quickly and efficiently as possible. 'We've been able to confirm that all three of our victims drank grapefruit juice produced by Squeeze The Day in the hours before they died. The fact of the matter is we don't know how many bottles of juice are affected, or where they've been contaminated. There could be any number of them out there, sitting in a warehouse, on shop shelves, or in people's fridges waiting to be drunk. For all we know, they could still be rolling off the production line. In terms of the investigation, all our efforts are going into narrowing down those possibilities, so we can isolate the affected products. What we need from you, Mike, is to help guide messaging and comms on this. We need to act swiftly, but we don't want to cause alarm or unnecessary damage.'

'No, that's right,' Mike said. 'From what you're saying, we don't yet know where suspicion lies in terms of the production line, do we?'

'Not yet,' Dexter replied.

'Or even if they definitely *have* been poisoned?'

'Correct.'

'Then we do need to exercise caution when it comes to public messaging. For example, if we were to come out and say "bottles of this particular brand of juice have been contaminated", that might not even be true, and if it is, it might not be anything to do with the brand or manufacturer. The contamination could've happened at the bottling plant they use, the warehouse they lease, the logistics company they use to transport it, the haulier who delivers it, the shopkeeper who sells it

— there are too many possible entry points here. I mean, I don't know how these things work, but it could even be feasible that something ended up in the lining of the cartons they use, or the lids used on the bottles. It could easily be nothing to do with the manufacturer at all, but you'd effectively collapse their business overnight. At the same time, from a public safety point of view it's crucial we minimise the chances of any more people coming into contact with contaminated products. That's where your team's tracing efforts will be vital.'

'Okay,' Caroline said, trying to take this all in. 'In terms of what we're doing, we've got three known cases. We're trying to trace the journey of each of those bottles of juice right back to source. We're speaking to the victims' friends and families to find out which shop they bought them from, then to the shopkeepers to find out which wholesaler they used, which haulier or courier delivered them, where those drivers picked up from, how the products got there in the first place — right the way back to the grapefruit tree, practically.'

'Perfect. If a pattern emerges, let me know straight away. It might be they all came via the same wholesaler, or they had the same delivery driver, they were all produced on a particular day or a specific line at the factory — whatever it is, we need to collate every possible piece of information about those bottles. Everyone who could've come into contact with them, every place they were left unattended. Even CCTV footage from the shops. There've been cases where people have randomly contaminated food and drink on the shelves in supermarkets.'

Caroline let out a heavy sigh. 'Christ. We don't need any more random elements thrown in here. There has to be a pattern somewhere along the line, sooner or later.'

'I don't think it's likely to have been done on the shelves,' Dexter said. 'We already know they were bought from three different retailers.'

Mike nodded. 'True, but it doesn't rule it out. There might be someone with a vendetta against the manufacturer, for example. They might've worked there in the past and been sacked, or had a relative who was. They could even have a personal grudge against the owners for a completely different reason. If you were to find the same character on CCTV at all three retailers in the days before those bottles were bought, you'd have a pattern and a suspect.'

'That's going to be a logistical impossibility,' Caroline said. 'Even if they'd been on the shelves for three days, you're looking at thirty or forty hours of footage per camera, per shop. And some poor bugger's going to have sit through all that and try to spot the same person cropping up on each of them.'

'And that's if we're lucky and have only three cases,'

Dexter added. 'We're going to need those extra troops, without a shadow of a doubt.'

'We also can't forget there's no actual confirmation of poisoning just at the moment,' Mike said. 'I understand it's looking that way, but until you've got toxicology results back we're treading a very thin line.'

'What about in the meantime?' Caroline asked. 'Would it be worth putting posters up in the shops, perhaps? "If you bought grapefruit juice from here, please return it" sort of thing?'

'Mmm, possibly,' Mike replied, not sounding entirely convinced. 'But I'm not sure it'd have much benefit. You'd be relying on people who've bought it to return to the same shop again, read the poster, make the connection and actually do something about it — all before they've gone to their fridge and drunk it. Contaminated bottles could've been bought and consumed by anyone, anywhere. They could be tourists, drivers passing through, people working away from home. Even if they *were* only contaminated in local shops, the bottles could still be all over the country.'

Caroline turned to Dexter. 'We'll need to liaise with other forces and cross-reference any similar cases or deaths on their patches.'

'Good shout,' Dexter said. 'I'll have a word with Aidan.'

Aidan was a trained HOLMES 2 user. The Home Office Large Major Enquiry System, which was first introduced in the mid-1980s and was later replaced by its second iteration in the early 2000s, was a national policing system that allowed local forces to log and collate information. It had proven vital in cracking major crimes that crossed county lines, whereas otherwise local forces tended to operate as satellites, with little cross-border consistency.

'What is it, Dex?' Caroline asked, noticing her colleague didn't seem entirely comfortable.

'I just get the feeling we're too many steps behind. We've already been cautious, and it's lost us time. If we carry on the same way, it won't be time that's lost. It'll be lives. We need to throw everything at it.'

'We are throwing everything at it,' Caroline replied. 'It's literally everything we have.'

'I know. And it's not enough. We need to go all out on the comms front. We've got to put out a full recall notice, surely? Radio, papers, social media, TV, the lot. I know you don't want to tread on any toes, but I think we'd be completely justified when you look at the circumstances. We know all three victims drank the same grapefruit juice from the same brand.'

'Ninety-nine percent of the bottles are probably fine, though,' Caroline said. 'It's a case of balancing risk against public hysteria. Plus we could end up with a massive lawsuit on our hands if it turns out the contamination happened further down the distribution line.'

'That doesn't change the fact we're well within our rights to put out a public message saying if you've bought this juice, return it and do not drink it. We're not saying it's the brand's fault. We're saying we can't guarantee its safety. Either way, it's a massive risk. If we do nothing, or not enough, and more people end up drinking the stuff and getting hurt — or worse — we could be dragged through the courts anyway. And I know I'd rather face a pissed-off company director than a family who's lost a loved one because of our negligence.'

'It's not negligence, Dex, it's caution.'

'Doesn't matter what it is, does it? It won't make that family feel any better.'

'It's a difficult balancing act,' Mike offered, trying to play the diplomat. 'All I can do is make recommendations, particularly while we don't have toxicology results, but ultimately it's an operational policing decision.'

Caroline sat silently and thought for a moment. These sorts of judgement calls were always an impossible ask. But Dexter was right: which of the two worst-case scenarios could she most easily have on her conscience? That was what it all boiled down to: choosing the option that best protected the public. After all, that's why they were in the job in the first place. And there were some elements of the job that media campaigns and corporate communications just couldn't beat.

'Okay,' she said. 'Mike, can you draft some materials? Don't publish anything yet, but let's get it ready to fire as soon as we've got confirmation from toxicology. Dex, you come with me to speak to the juice company's owner. If Sara and Aidan are working on the trail from the bottom up, we'll go top down. The odds are the contamination has happened at the factory. In any case, you can't beat looking at the whites of people's eyes, can you?'

24

Caroline and Dexter arrived outside the premises of Squeeze The Day a short while later, keen not to waste any time. Caroline had phoned ahead as Dexter drove, to make sure somebody senior would be available.

'Bit smaller than I expected,' Dexter said as he switched off the engine.

'Just goes to show the power of a good branding consultant, I suppose.'

Caroline stepped out of the car, walked up to the intercom buzzer on the front of the building, and pressed the button.

'Hello?'

'DI Hills and DS Antoine from Rutland Police, here to see Alistair Fletcher. We phoned a few minutes ago.'

'Ah yes. Come through.'

A buzzing sound indicated the door was unlocked,

and the pair headed inside. A few moments later, a door at the far end of the corridor opened and a woman in her late fifties approached them.

'Hi, I'm Debbie,' she said, shaking their hands. 'Follow me, I'll take you upstairs.'

They followed Debbie along the corridor and up a set of stairs, which opened onto a long landing. On one side, a floor-to-ceiling window allowed them to see the full production line on the factory floor below. On the other, a series of doors led to what Caroline presumed were offices of some sort.

A few doors along, Debbie stopped, knocked on one and opened the door, before stepping aside for them.

As Caroline and Dexter entered, Alistair Fletcher stood up from behind his desk.

'Hi. Thanks for not coming in a marked car,' he said, before gesturing to Debbie that she could close the door and leave. 'You know how people can get if they see a couple of coppers rocking up. Rumours spread like wildfire round here. How can I help?'

Caroline forced a smile. If Fletcher was worried about a police car being seen in the vicinity of his premises, he wasn't going to enjoy the journey from here on in.

'It's actually quite a tricky subject,' she said. 'We're investigating the deaths of three people in the local area who all died very suddenly, despite being relatively fit and healthy. The only connection we can find at the moment is that they all drank your grapefruit juice in the hours before their deaths.'

Caroline watched as Alistair Fletcher's face turned white. For a brief moment, she wondered if they were looking at their fourth victim.

'Jesus,' he whispered, a tremble in his voice. 'What, are you sure? I don't know what you're saying. I don't know how that's even possible. I mean, its just grapefruit juice. We've got really high safety standards. We've won awards and everything.'

'We're not saying anything,' Caroline replied. 'We don't know what's happened. All we know so far is they'd all drunk your juice. We believe it may have been tampered with at some point. We just need to find out where and how.'

'Sorry, yes. Of course I'll do everything I can to help. It's just come as such a shock. The first thing that crosses my mind is that this could ruin my business. Well, not my first thought, of course. But you know what I mean. I hope.'

'Of course,' Caroline said, trying to placate Fletcher, who was clearly shaken by the news.

'That authentic?' Dexter asked pointing to a framed, signed football shirt on the wall of the office.

'Hundred percent,' Fletcher replied. 'Signed by the title winning squad from twenty-sixteen. And Ranieri. That's his on the sleeve there. Looks more like a logo from a posh clothing company in London, doesn't it? Classy to his core, that guy.'

'Italians for you. How'd you get hold of this?'

'Mate of mine works at the academy. You go to games?'

'When I get time, yeah. Blimey, it must be worth a fortune.'

'You'd be surprised,' Fletcher said. 'A dealer offered me eight hundred quid. They sign millions of the buggers, those players. Everyone thinks they've got something really rare or unique, and they're convinced it's worth more. So when they're offered a few hundred quid, they turn it down and hang onto it, which then makes it rarer and pushes the price up when someone does want to sell.'

'Which then brings everyone else out of the woodwork wanting to sell, which pushes the price back down,' Dexter replied, smiling. 'That's the collectables game for you.'

'Same with antiques,' Fletcher said. 'Although I did check eBay the other day and one of these was up there for thirteen-hundred quid. Full certificates and everything, mind. Doubt my mate Matt's going to knock one of those up on A4 for me.'

With Alistair Fletcher now seeming less nervous and a little more on comfortable ground, Caroline tried to bring the conversation back round to more important matters.

'Look, we don't want to cause any disruption or problems for your business, I promise you. But the fact of the matter is three people have lost their lives, and our concern is there could be more to come. Until we find out where the contamination has occurred and are confident it's isolated, there's no knowing who could be at risk. It could even be your own family,' she said, nodding towards a photograph propped up against the computer monitor, of Fletcher with his wife and two children.

Fletcher gave a small sigh. 'You don't need to play that card. I know how serious this is. I'm feeling that more than you, because it's so close to home. I'm as devastated for the families of the people who've died as you are, plus I've got the added pressure of worrying about the people I employ — and their families. And that's before we even get onto my own. Any downtime would kill us. Especially if business is going to nosedive because people think all our bloody drinks are poisoned.'

'On the plus side, if people aren't buying the juice, the production downtime won't matter so much,' Dexter said with a wry smile. 'Sorry. Poor taste.'

'So was that,' Fletcher replied with a harrumph.

'The sooner we can get to the bottom of this, and with minimal fuss, the better,' Caroline said. 'If you're able to cooperate with us, we can reduce the impact on you and your business as much as possible.'

'And if I didn't, you'd be able to force me to anyway, right?'

Caroline cocked her head in mock consideration. 'This is a triple manslaughter investigation at best, and I'm certainly not making threats, but yes, we could have the factory shut down completely while we take the place apart. That'd be far more disruptive, expensive and time-consuming for everybody. It's not a route I'd particularly want to go down, if I'm honest.'

Fletcher murmured to himself. 'No, me neither. So what can I do?'

'We'd like to bring experts in to inspect the machinery and the process. In the meantime, we'll need full CCTV archives from the premises. Is it all backed up?'

Fletcher rubbed his chin. 'Well, yeah. We don't do it all ourselves, though. We've got a company that installed it and maintains it. I'd have to speak to their technician and find out how we can get hold of that for you. How far back do you need to go?'

'As far as we can, ideally. If we can have the full backups, that'll make life much easier. That way we'll know we haven't missed anything.'

'Alright,' Fletcher said, nodding. 'I'll give them a bell now.'

Almost as if cued by the mention of a phone call, Caroline's own mobile started to ring. Taking it out of her pocket to silence it, she saw Mark's name on the screen.

'Okay if I leave this with you for a sec?' she said to Dexter and Alistair Fletcher, suddenly realising how long it'd been since she'd given Mark an update. Behind her instinctive guilt were further worries — what if something had happened? What if one of the kids was unwell? 'I'll be back in a few minutes. I'll go and take this outside.'

Answering the call and putting the phone to her ear, Caroline stood and left the office.

25

'I really can't say for certain,' Caroline said as she paced the small parking area in front of the industrial unit. 'Things are moving so quickly, which is good, because we're already close to a breakthrough, but it does mean I've not even had thirty seconds to work out timings and things. I'm really sorry. I've just had my head buried in getting this all done and handed over as quickly as possible so I can get back to you all.'

She heard Mark sigh at the other end of the phone. 'You said you'd be back by tonight. When you called yesterday to say you wouldn't be back then, I mean.'

'I know. I know. I'm sorry. We're told the results should be back tomorrow.'

'You told me yesterday the results would be back today.'

'Those were different results. We've had to order extra tests, and... Look, I can't go into it or say any more. I wish I could.'

'But I thought the whole point of going back was to hand over to Dexter and get extra bodies in so you wouldn't be needed. Why can't he wait for the results instead?'

'Yeah. Yeah, I know. Unfortunately that's taking a bit of time.'

She'd already updated Chief Superintendent Arnold by phone on their way over to Squeeze The Day, confirming to him they were looking at three cases of — at best — manslaughter, and potentially murder. The difference would come in being able to prove an intention to kill. Without a suspect, or even a definite idea of what had happened, that was still some way off.

'How long?' Mark asked. 'Really, I mean.' He wore his heart on his sleeve, and Caroline was usually pretty good at being able to decode his thoughts and emotions, but now he seemed a little more guarded than usual. She couldn't tell if he was disappointed, angry or resigned. A part of her worried it was all three.

'I don't know. I wish I did. I'm not being evasive. I just don't want to make any promises and end up breaking them again. I'm doing everything I can to get back as quickly as possible, but I can't just leave. Things are moving, though. Arnold seems to have my back on it. He started the ball rolling pretty much immediately, so we couldn't have gone much faster if we'd wanted to. And I'll be able to get the time back plus extra, so we can have a longer holiday in the summer. A proper one.'

'The boys miss you.'

Caroline sighed. 'I know. I miss them too. All of you.'

'This wasn't meant to happen again.'

'It hasn't. And it won't. No-one could've seen this case coming, Mark. I can't really talk about it at the moment, but I will. You'll just have to trust me for now. I'm really sorry.'

Mark was silent for a few moments. 'Yeah,' he said eventually. 'So am I.'

'Believe me, I'm getting out of here and back to you all the second I'm able to. And when we're back from holiday I'll be making sure we're properly resourced in the long-term, because you're absolutely right, we can't keep doing this.'

'Come off it, Caz. You know that's not going to happen. It's not like big cases crop up every week, is it? I get how these things work. It's budgets. They're not going to have people sitting around doing nothing for most of the year.'

'No, but there are things that can be done. They can put things in place so next time we only need to push a button and we can have extras seconded in straight away, without all the paperwork and bureaucracy. And like you said, these things don't crop up every week. It's not like London, Mark. I'm not working all the hours God sends. I don't have to, most of the time. But when something kicks off, we're very much up against it.'

'Maybe recently,' Mark said. Something in his voice told Caroline he was leaning towards resignation.

'What's that meant to mean?' she asked.

'I mean you've not been working all hours recently. But you were before. Since we moved to Rutland, I mean. It doesn't matter where you are. It's your natural state.'

'That's not fair. Yes, I'm dedicated to my job. But I'm even more dedicated to you and the kids, which is why things have changed.'

'Have they, though? Or were you just lying low for a few months to keep everyone happy? I've seen how distant you get, Caz. I'm not daft. At times you're like an addict who's not had a fix. You get itchy. Then the second a juicy case pops up, you're off and we're second best again. Jesus Christ, we were on holiday. Some of us still are. It's not normal, Caz.'

'Nothing's normal in this job. Not round here, anyway.'

'Then maybe it's not the right job.'

Caroline let out a noise that sounded and felt like she'd been punched in the gut. 'Don't say that. Of course it is. It's what I do. Who I am. What else do you want me to do? Work in a flipping gift shop in Oakham? Maybe I could be a farmer, or stroke ospreys or whatever the hell it is everyone else does round here. I'm a public servant, Mark. I help keep people safe. Including you and the kids.'

Mark let out a loud sigh. 'We are safe. We're safer than we've ever been. We're talking about Rutland, for crying out loud. It's not the sodding Bronx. You don't need to do your Cagney and Lacey thing anymore. That's what Enron are there for.'

'They're called EMSOU.'

'It doesn't matter what they're called. Why can't you just stick to tractor thefts and cattle rustling and let them take care of the big stuff?'

'Oh thanks. Thanks a lot. I'm sorry my job is so inconvenient for you, Mark. Why doesn't the little lady just do the easy stuff instead, eh? Maybe I can see if anyone needs a secretary. Perhaps then you won't feel so threatened.'

Caroline regretted her words almost as soon as she'd said them.

'Threatened?' Mark replied. 'Is that really what you think of me?'

'You know it isn't.'

'I don't know if I do. I don't know anything anymore, Caz. At least in London we knew what was what. Things weren't great. Far from it. But at least we knew why. It made sense that you were distant. That's what the Met does to people. But now we haven't got that justification, and you're still the same. Nothing seems to makes sense anymore.'

Caroline didn't know for certain where this conversation was headed, but she didn't like the sound of it.

'Mark, it's a one-off. Things are so much better than they were in London. You know that. The boys are happy. They're safe. I'm working far less than I was. Yes, it can be unpredictable at times, but like I said, I'm making sure measures are in place to stop that affecting us again in the future.'

For a short while, Mark didn't respond. It was probably only seconds, but to Caroline it felt like hours.

'How do I know that?' he said eventually. 'I know you'll tell me to trust you, but that's always your answer, isn't it? Just believe you, just have faith, just pipe down and put up with it and hope for the best.'

'That's not it at all.'

'It is, though, isn't it? It's easier to bury it into the background and hope it'll go away. But it never does. Rutland was meant to be a fresh start for us. A new beginning. But the longer things go on, the more I find myself wanting to be back in London. It might not be physically safer, but at least emotionally I knew where I was.'

'We can't go back to London, Mark.'

'I know *we* can't.' Mark's voice was almost a whisper. 'And I know you won't.'

Caroline could feel her heart hammering in her chest. 'Come on. Think about this. We've got nothing in London anymore.'

Although she didn't quite voice it, the meaning was clear. Mark's mum had passed away suddenly a few months earlier, and his dad and brother had died before they moved to Rutland — both from cancer. Caroline knew her own battle with the disease had had more of an impact on her husband than she'd realised at the time, and it had been one of the reasons she'd kept it from him for so long. All she'd ever done was try to protect them, and each time she'd managed to get it wrong.

'What do you think of when you think of home?' Mark asked.

'How do you mean?'

'What comes into your head? When I say home.'

'Our house, of course. It's literally our home.'

'Yeah. Literally. But it doesn't feel like home. Not when you're so distant from me. When you're around, when you're present, we could be anywhere. It'd feel happy and safe wherever we were. But when you disappear off into your head, or get bogged down with work or wherever it is you go mentally, I feel like I'm left on my own. And at that point all I want is familiar surroundings.'

'You want us to move back to London?'

'I don't know. I don't know what I want *us* to do, Caz. That's the problem.'

Caroline swallowed. 'We can't have this talk now, Mark. It's something we need to do face-to-face.'

'Whenever that'll be.'

'It'll be soon. Very soon. I promise.'

'You can't promise. You know you can't.'

'Yes I can,' she replied, her jaw tight. 'I absolutely can. And I am.' Even through the phone, the atmosphere was clear. Mark didn't believe her, and in any case, even if he did, it was a promise she knew she couldn't keep — and certainly couldn't break. 'I'll call you later, okay? The sooner I get this done, the sooner we can all be together again.'

Once the call had ended, Caroline took a moment to compose herself, then headed back into the factory. She could feel her hands shaking, her legs like jelly as she took deep breaths and tried to focus on the task in hand.

Reaching the top of the stairs, she walked back down the corridor towards Alistair Fletcher's office and opened the door. Dexter was alone inside, his head cocked at an unnatural angle as he tried to decipher the scribbles on the Leicester City football shirt.

'Dex. Where's Fletcher?' she asked.

'He's gone to speak to the security people about the CCTV. He'll be back in a minute. Here, who do you reckon this one is? It's got a twenty-six underneath it. Mahrez was number twenty-six, wasn't he?'

'I don't know. Where'd he go, Dex?'

'Man City.'

'I'm talking about Fletcher. Which way did he go?'

Dexter turned around, a look of mild confusion on his face. 'I don't know,' he said. 'Out the door and right, I think.'

'Why the hell did you let him out of your sight? He's the closest thing we've got to a suspect, and he could've gone anywhere or done anything. You'd better pray he hasn't. Follow me.'

Dexter followed Caroline out of the room and back into the corridor. As they did so, a door opened and Alistair Fletcher stepped out, visibly surprised to see them standing right in front of him.

'Everything okay?' he asked. 'There hasn't been another one, has there?'

'No,' Caroline replied. 'Not that we're aware of. Any news on the CCTV?'

Fletcher looked at each of them in turn before speaking. 'Uh, mixed bag. We've got footage going back a month, I'm told. It's a rolling twenty-eight-day archive. The only problem is one of the zones has been down for a little while, so the cameras in that zone don't have any recordings. The others are all fine, though.'

Caroline clenched her jaw as she felt Dexter shuffling uncomfortably beside her.

'Which zone is that?' she asked, fearing she already knew the answer.

Fletcher swallowed before he spoke. 'The production lines,' he said.

26

Two hours later, Caroline watched as Dexter sat on the chair in her office, across the desk from her. He looked disconsolate.

'Boss, I don't know what to say. I'm so sorry.'

'I can well imagine you are,' Caroline replied. 'What on earth were you thinking?'

Dexter shrugged. 'I clearly wasn't. I dunno. I was just looking at the shirt, and he only went to make a phone call. I don't think I even registered you'd gone somewhere different. I took my eye off the ball. I don't have an excuse. I know it's all on me. I completely understand if you want to drop me from the case or take it on yourself.'

Caroline sighed. 'You know we don't have enough bodies as it is. We can't afford to lose you. And in case you hadn't remembered, I'm meant to be on holiday.

The last thing I want is to risk my marriage because you got hypnotised by a bloody football shirt.'

Dexter gave a sigh of relief. 'Do we have any news on reinforcements?' he asked.

'It's happening. We might struggle for CID, but we've got uniform going through the CCTV. With a month's worth of footage, there's plenty to keep them going. Even if we are missing half of it.'

Dexter's head dropped. 'I really am sorry, boss.'

'I know. But there's not much we can do now, other than work with what we've got. And, as it happens, you might have inadvertently given us something.'

'Oh?'

'We managed to put some pressure on the technician to find out what happened to the missing zone. We mentioned we'd have our IT forensics people on it, and that we'd find out exactly how the footage got lost. We cut him a plea bargain, and he confirmed that the zone covering the production area had been working fine, but that Fletcher specifically asked him over the phone to disable it and delete the archive footage.'

'Jesus Christ. Fletcher knows there was something on it. That's perverting the course of justice.'

'I'm well aware of that. He's already been brought in for a formal interview.'

'What's he playing at? It's got to be him, hasn't it? He's our man. He's guaranteed a prison sentence for deleting the footage as it is. You don't risk that unless you think it'll get you off something bigger.'

Caroline murmured her agreement. 'Potentially. Or he might be covering for someone else. Not everyone realises the extent of the law, or what traces are left when things are deleted. He might have panicked and not thought about it. And even if he did, we don't know for certain he was weighing one prison sentence up against another. Maybe the alternative was far worse than that.'

'I guess. He seemed pretty petrified of losing his business.'

'Exactly. People do daft things. We see it all the time.'

'Or he could've been blackmailed by someone.'

Caroline nodded. 'It's a line we'll run with in the interview. We'll give him the option as an out.'

Among many techniques and strategies used in police interviews, this was one that was often successful. In a situation where a suspect was flat-out denying their involvement, or where the police knew something had happened but needed the suspect's co-operation, providing them with an off-ramp tended to yield positive results. Too many suspects boxed themselves into dead-ends or felt cornered by the police's line of questioning, in which case they tended to simply shut down. Suggesting that perhaps it was possible they'd been coerced, or made to act against their will, provided a hugely attractive avenue for the suspect. Psychologically speaking, pretty much everyone felt more comfortable with the truth. But when that came up against the threat of a loss of liberty or admitting guilt, a metaphorical wall went up. By giving the suspect a chance to — at least mostly — explain the truth but still avoid direct responsibility, things started to move very quickly. And even if they were purely using it as an opportunity to shift the blame onto someone else, that could be swiftly disproven as part of what followed.

'In fact,' Caroline continued, 'I think we should put our heads together and plan our strategy for Fletcher's interview.'

'Me?' Dexter asked, seeming genuinely surprised to be involved.

'Yes, you. I want you in there with me.'

'Wow. Okay. Thanks. I half-expected to be sent home, if I'm honest.'

Caroline let out a small laugh. 'Like I said, Dex, we can't afford to lose anyone right now. You're a brilliant detective and a good interviewer. Anyway, we already know Fletcher sees you as a bit of a patsy. We can use that to our advantage.'

Dexter looked at Caroline and forced a smile.

27

Caroline and Dexter headed into the interview room, where Alistair Fletcher and his solicitor were waiting for them.

The detectives had prepared their plan of action. Circumstances and a lack of clear evidence dictated it would be more exploratory than anything, but things were moving fast, and there was a good chance the rest of the team would discover something while the interviews were ongoing.

The first interview with a suspect almost always sought to establish the facts, regardless of what evidence the police had. It was no use wading in with a file full of photographs and witness statements, because that would only cause the suspect to freeze and clam up. By asking them the basics — where where you? What do you know? What did you see? — they gave the suspect enough rope to hang themselves, as well as providing themselves extra time before the second interview to make their rebuttals watertight and categorically disprove what they'd said in the first.

Fletcher's solicitor cut a steely figure as he sat next to his client, opposite Caroline and Dexter. She could tell he was new to the job. Apart from the fact he looked no older than twelve, he seemed to have the enthusiasm and fervour of a man who'd not yet buckled under the onslaught of repetitive police interviews and legal aid work.

Caroline started the recording and read out the names of everyone present.

'Alistair, you're being interviewed under police caution today in connection with the deaths of Barbara Patchett, Luke Grennan and Faith Pearson. Do you know those people?'

'No,' Fletcher replied.

'Have you ever heard of any of them?'

'Not until you told me about them, no.'

'Do you know how they died?'

Fletcher swallowed. 'From what you told me, they were poisoned.'

'That's looking highly likely. Post-mortem results also showed each of the three had drunk grapefruit juice earlier on the day they died. Does your company make grapefruit juice?'

'Yes.'

'We know each of them bought and drank your grapefruit juice before they died. Do you know of any way in which that might have caused them harm?'

Caroline and Dexter watched as the gravity of the situation appeared to dawn on Fletcher again.

'No. No, I don't see how that's even possible.'

'Perhaps you could talk us through the process of producing your grapefruit juice. I imagine there are quite a few different people involved, and potentially various opportunities for someone to tamper with the product?'

'Well, yes. I mean, you saw for yourself how much goes on even just in our little factory. It's not like I sit there hand-squeezing fruits into bottles and dropping them off at shops. Even after they leave us, there's god knows how many places the products could be tampered with. There's distributors, couriers, shopkeepers. All sorts. There could even be someone fiddling with them on the shelves.'

'I can assure you we're considering all possibilities,' Dexter said. 'And we'll be investigating the whole supply chain. We know there are lots of ways this could have happened, but we're going to find out how. I'm sure you want us to get to the bottom of it so your business doesn't suffer.'

'Yes. Of course.'

'Naturally, we have to start somewhere. And it

makes sense to start at the top of the chain, rather than the bottom.'

'Not if all three people bought the juice from the same shop, it's not,' Fletcher replied, as if they hadn't considered the possibility.

'They didn't,' Caroline said, watching his face carefully. It looked as if the faintest glimmer of hope had been extinguished from behind the man's eyes. 'Now, I'm sure you understand that in order to get to the bottom of what happened, we need to collect evidence. That way we can build up a picture and prove what's happened, so the guilty party can be prosecuted. When we asked you for access to the CCTV archives, you told us the zone that covered the production lines hadn't been active, so there was no footage covering that area. Why was that?'

Fletcher gave a small shrug. 'I don't know. Some sort of error on the system. Maybe it hadn't been set up properly.'

'It's a pretty crucial part of the building to cover, isn't it? I'd say from a safety and security point of view, that's the bit I'd want to make sure *was* working.'

'Me too,' Fletcher replied. 'It would've made this a whole lot easier. I'm hardly going to wipe the footage and make myself look dodgy, am I?'

'We never said you had. But you're right. It really doesn't help you at all. Because while we're not able to identify the culprit, it's your business that'll suffer.

Especially if anyone else drinks contaminated grapefruit juice produced in your factory.'

'I know. I get that. But I can't help that the CCTV was on the blink, can I?'

Caroline looked at Fletcher, and in her head she made a decision. She'd tried to give the man an out. She'd provided him plenty of opportunities to admit what they already knew — that he'd ordered the deletion of the footage — and she was no longer prepared to err on the side of caution for him. To hell with the man. As soon as the first interview was over, she'd give the nod for the media messaging to go out, warning the public not to drink juice produced by his company, and to bring any bottles or cartons to the police for inspection.

'That all depends,' she said. 'The trouble is, it's at best slowing down our identification of the culprit. It could even scupper it completely. And ultimately, as the company's sole owner, it's you who's responsible for making sure the products you produce are safe for consumption. If we don't find the culprit, I'm afraid the buck stops with you and we'd be looking at corporate manslaughter charges.'

Fletcher's face turned a pale shade of grey as the realisation set in.

'And to be honest, Alistair, that's probably the best case scenario as things stand right now. Because if we're not looking at carelessness and negligence, the only other alternative is that the footage on that CCTV system was deliberately wiped. And then we're looking at something altogether more sinister. That'd be perverting the course of justice, which carries a maximum sentence of life in prison.'

Caroline locked eyes with Fletcher, watching as he quietly considered his options.

'Is there anything you want to tell us at this stage?' she asked.

Fletcher swallowed hard and blinked a few times before answering. 'No,' he replied quietly.

Caroline slowly nodded, then gave a smile. 'Alright. Good.'

28

Caroline had barely slept a wink that night, knowing there was every chance toxicology results on Barbara Patchett could be returned the following day. She felt certain that as soon as poisoning was scientifically confirmed, Alistair Fletcher's whole house of cards would come crashing down. The investigation would then move into a new phase, which would be less restricted by time and resources.

Fortunately for her nerves, the email landed in her inbox mere minutes after she'd arrived in the office. As the printer whirred into life behind her, she scan-read the results on the screen in front of her. Moments later, she grabbed the paper from the printer and assembled her team in the main incident room.

'Okay, they're in,' she said, holding the report in front of her.

'Atropine?' Aidan asked.

Caroline looked at him, puzzled. 'Why do you say that?'

'It's Sara's theory, not mine. And she's rarely wrong.'

Caroline thought she detected a hint of a smile from Aidan towards his younger colleague, but that was a thought for another time.

'I was doing a bit of research when I got home last night,' Sara said. 'In my own time, I mean. I was looking up the symptoms and what forms of poisoning might cause them. There were a few, but atropine seemed most likely. Apparently it causes flushing, tachycardia, fever and urinary problems. Interestingly, it usually stops people urinating, but not always. Something to do with the parasympathetic nervous system, which stimulates the muscle in the wall of the bladder. Atropine's used to help control bladder issues, but in an extremely high dose it can do the opposite, especially if there's an existing health condition or interaction with other medication.'

'Like blood pressure meds,' Aidan added.

Caroline took a deep breath. 'Well, you've rather taken the wind out of my sails there, Sara. But you're right. Extremely high levels of atropine were found in Barbara Patchett's body. It's not something that'd find its way naturally into bottles of juice, but apparently it is a very bitter substance. Perfect for hiding in a drink that's already bitter. Like grapefruit juice, for example. Ladies and gents, I think we've got our culprit.'

29

Caroline took some deep breaths and tried to calm her nerves as she waited on the other end of the phone. She'd never enjoyed the occasional media duties that came with major investigations, but sometimes it had to be done. She knew she had to focus on the content of what she was saying and the message she was trying to get across, rather than worrying about how she sounded or what people might be thinking, but that was easier said than done.

She listened as a pop song she'd never heard of came to an end, and the presenter, Rob Persani, started to speak.

'That's Drake here on Rutland and Stamford Sound. Now, police in Rutland have warned of a potentially serious contamination of fruit juice supplied to retailers and consumers in the local area, and are asking the public to be vigilant. Detective Inspector Caroline Hills from Rutland Police joins me on the line now. Detective Inspector, this is quite a serious matter, isn't it?'

'It's extremely serious, yes,' Caroline replied, quelling her nerves by slipping into professional mode. 'We believe we're looking at a very serious form of contamination here, and we're urging the general public to take extreme caution. In fact, we believe there could be a potential risk to life as a result of drinking contaminated fruit juice.'

'Wow. We're talking very serious, then. So what should the public be looking out for?'

'At the moment, we believe the contamination has been contained to only one product, which is grapefruit juice produced by Squeeze The Day. And it's important to be clear about that, because we don't want to cause any confusion around other juice companies, who aren't involved in this case.'

'When you say "involved", are we looking at something deliberate as opposed to an accident of some sort?'

Caroline felt her heart lurch in her chest. 'We're keeping all possibilities in mind at the moment, especially while our investigation is still ongoing, but right now our main focus is on making sure the public are aware that if they have, or come across grapefruit juice manufactured by Squeeze The Day, they should absolutely not drink it or consume it in any way, and should contact the police non-emergency number, which is 101, so we can arrange to have it collected for testing.'

'And what if there are people listening who have perhaps drunk this juice recently? What should they be aware of or looking out for?'

'I think in general my advice would be not to panic, but to be extra vigilant of any symptoms, and if you do feel unwell, you should go straight to your nearest accident and emergency department with the bottle or container you drank from. And if you've been ill or unwell recently after having drunk Squeeze The Day's grapefruit juice, again we'd ask you to call the police non-emergency number on 101, so we can provide advice.'

'But in the meantime, don't drink Squeeze The Day grapefruit juice.'

'That's correct,' Caroline replied.

30

Caroline sat down opposite Alistair Fletcher in the interview room for the second time.

By now, she knew he was lying through his teeth. The CCTV technician had sung like a canary, and confirmed that Fletcher had asked him to wipe the footage. With Fletcher having denied this on record in a police interview, they now had evidence that he'd been lying.

They still hadn't uncovered any links between Fletcher and the victims. It appeared there was only one link anywhere: the history between Luke Grennan and Faith Pearson. Although Caroline didn't like to put things down to coincidence, even she had to concede that was the most likely explanation.

The absence of a direct link between Fletcher and the victims made it unlikely he'd been the one putting atropine in the juice, Caroline thought. After all, what would be the point? He risked losing everything and gaining nothing. The fact that he'd incriminated himself over the CCTV footage told her a lot, too. If Alistair Fletcher had masterminded some great poisoning plot, he would've disabled the CCTV beforehand — not panicked and rung the technician to delete it for him.

This all led Caroline to believe Fletcher was covering for someone. She was sure they'd find out who eventually, but time was not on her side. She'd had confirmation that the computer forensics experts believed they could retrieve the data and footage, but it wouldn't be an easy job. They had explained it to her, but she hadn't fully understood the detail. As far as she could gather, digital files were never truly deleted; they were simply no longer referenced. Over time, newer files and fragments took their place and overwrote them, but if the storage drive was salvaged quickly enough, that damage could be minimised.

'Okay, Alistair,' she said as she opened Fletcher's second interview. 'We want to take this opportunity to clear up a few details from your interview earlier today. Before we begin, is there anything you wanted to add?'

Fletcher looked at his solicitor, then back at Caroline before shaking his head. 'No.'

'Alright. So I just want to run over a few of the details with you. You told us that when you called the CCTV technician to obtain the footage from the production line, he told you the zone covering that area was faulty and hadn't been recording, is that correct?'

Fletcher hesitated for a moment. 'Yes.'

'Did you ask him to delete the footage, Alistair?'

Fletcher's solicitor leaned across. 'You don't have to answer that.'

Fletcher looked back at Caroline and Dexter. 'No. No, I didn't.'

'Are you sure?' Caroline asked. 'Because we spoke to the technician, and he's provided us with a statement claiming that you called him and specifically asked him to wipe all archived footage of the production line zone for security reasons.'

Fletcher stayed silent.

'Did you do that, Alistair?' Caroline asked.

'No,' came the reply.

'Why would he lie about that?'

'I don't know.'

'He said you sounded agitated. Frantic, almost. What were you worried about, Alistair?'

The solicitor leaned across and whispered in Fletcher's ear.

'No comment,' came the reply.

'What was on the footage that you didn't want us to see?'

'No comment.'

'Do you know what was on the footage?'

'No comment.'

'We've had toxicology results back on one of the people who died after drinking your juice, Alistair. Extremely high levels of atropine were found in their bodies. Do you know anything about atropine?'

'No comment.'

'It's highly poisonous. Ten or twenty milligrams can incapacitate somebody. A hundred milligrams can kill. Significantly more was found in the body of Barbara Patchett. She will have died very quickly indeed, as our other two victims appear to have done. As I understand it, atropine's a very bitter substance. Difficult to hide, especially in a dose the size they ingested. Did the CCTV footage show you injecting atropine into bottles of grapefruit juice?'

'No. No comment.'

'Where did you get the atropine from, Alistair?'

Fletcher looked at his solicitor, his eyes almost pleading. 'I didn't,' he said. 'It wasn't me.'

'Who was it?'

Fletcher looked down at the table. 'No comment.'

'Has someone coerced you into doing this?'

'No comment.'

'Have they blackmailed you?'

A beat. 'No comment.'

Caroline leaned forward, closing the gap between them.

'Alistair, if you've been blackmailed or coerced into covering for someone, that simply isn't fair or right. You don't need to face life in prison for something you didn't do. We can help you. I know these people can be very convincing, and tell you they'll do all sorts of things to you and your family if you grass them up, but there's a reason they have to say those things. They're empty threats. We can protect you, as long as you give us the truth.'

Fletcher swallowed. 'I've told you the truth.'

31

Jack Hayward poked a swollen finger at the remote control and switched the channel. He couldn't stand watching the news. Even the theme tune gave him the heebie-jeebies. There was always some sort of death or destruction going on. They never talked about any of the good stuff.

Jack struggled to look on the bright side of life as it was. It wasn't easy to be positive and bubbly when you were confined to a chair for every waking hour. He'd lost count of the illnesses and ailments the doctors told him he had. He'd stopped listening after a while. Nothing but bad news.

He looked at the clock on his mantelpiece and calculated how long it'd be before Veronica popped in. There wasn't much else to do but count down. To what, he didn't know. It was good to see a familiar face when he didn't have much else, but he had to admit he wasn't all that keen on her. It was nice that she popped in twice a day, but he wondered how much effort she'd put in if she wasn't conveniently on her way to or from work, or if their front doors weren't two feet apart.

He chastised himself silently for thinking that way. He'd be even grumpier if she didn't pop in. He supposed he should be grateful, but it was difficult when he didn't feel he had much to be grateful for. As much as he appreciated Veronica's unimpressive efforts, he'd much rather not need them in the first place. He'd been happier and more appreciative when he'd had his health, he thought, before realising he hadn't been appreciative in the slightest. Perhaps he should've been, he pondered.

He leaned across to his side table, feeling his back creaking as he did, and carefully took the clingfilm off the sandwiches Veronica had left out for him that morning. He took a bite from one and grimaced. He had no idea what she'd put in them, but it tasted foul.

He threw the remains of the sandwich at the plate and swallowed, hoping the taste would disappear quickly. No such luck. Glancing back at the side table, he saw the bottle Veronica had left next to the plate of sandwiches. Some poncy organic juice she'd spotted in one of her daft health food shops. He'd much rather wash down the vomit sandwiches with a nice pint of mild, but he supposed this would have to do. It certainly couldn't be any worse.

He opened the bottle and sniffed. Grapefruit. Not so bad, as far as fruits went — which wasn't far in Jack's book. He opened his mouth and took a few big swigs, swilling the juice around his mouth in an attempt to purge the taste of the sandwich. He'd have to have a word with her about that. It just wasn't on.

By the time he felt confident enough to see if the taste had gone, he'd already downed half the bottle. It tasted better than the sandwiches, but not by much. After a few more swigs, he put the juice back down on the table and returned to the television.

32

Alistair Fletcher moved his jaw in small circles as he tried to relieve the tension. It was difficult not to feel tense. Whichever direction he turned, he was stuffed. It hadn't taken him long to work out what had gone on. As soon as the police had told him about the deaths, it all fell into place. He hadn't known immediately what he was going to do, but that had soon become clear in his mind.

The police interviews had been horrendous. He'd never been in a situation like that before. He wanted to hope he'd never have the pleasure again either, but he knew that wouldn't be the case. Next time, he hoped, things would go a little more smoothly.

Although the next step was clear in his mind, there were two ways it could go from there. It could work, or it could not. Assuming it did, he'd have a choice to make. Faced with a long stretch inside for perverting the course of justice, the decision seemed a lot easier than it otherwise might have done, but his solicitor had been very reassuring. Although the police had made a big song and dance about the maximum sentence being life in prison, his solicitor told him this was designed to scare him into revealing everything, and that the usual sentence handed out for perverting the course of justice could easily be as little as four months. It would be foolish to expect a sentence that light, especially when it was connected with manslaughter or even murder, but a year or two wouldn't be the end of the world.

Whichever way he looked at it, life had changed irrevocably. His business was gone. There was no doubt about that. Things had been tight as it was, and there was no way they could weather a public safety campaign that told people not to buy their products. That wasn't the sort of thing the company could ever recover from. The business was gone, and he would be spending some time inside. The best he could hope for was a minimal sentence and to come out of this in the most positive way manageable.

He knew there was a possibility the police would be able to retrieve the CCTV footage. And even if they didn't, he was certain there'd be plenty of other evidence that would lead them directly to their killer without him having to breathe a word. Ultimately, his silence was his biggest bargaining chip. If his next move went to plan, as long as he kept shtum, and as long as the police *did* still get their man without him having to break his silence, that would be the best outcome possible.

He hadn't told his solicitor any of this, of course. He'd told him he'd simply panicked. The business had been struggling — that was easily provable — and when the police had turned up and told him three people had died because of contaminated juice, it had terrified and frightened him, and his immediate instinct had been to protect his staff and his family. And if he was careful, it would be impossible to prove otherwise.

He wasn't sure the police had bought it. At the end of the day, it was their job to assume suspicion and get someone in a cell. But they must have been at least pretty certain he wasn't the one who was responsible for the deaths. They'd let him out on bail before his clock had run down, and hadn't applied for an extension — all things his solicitor told him they were perfectly entitled to do, and which he should reasonably expect them to do. He wondered if this meant they were confident in retrieving the deleted CCTV footage, or if they'd discovered additional evidence which meant Alistair was now small fry to them. He hoped so, anyway. He'd have his day in court soon enough, but until then he was as free as could be, save for having to register at the police station each week and not being able to leave the country.

The beauty of dark evenings was twofold. It was always quiet round there, but doubly so at night. If anyone or anything were out of place, he'd know about it. He knew there was a chance the police would be watching him in some way. He'd seen plenty of crime dramas in which they let the suspect go, smirking to himself and thinking he was free, only to walk straight into the police's waiting arms five minutes later when he tried to do something stupid.

There was no doubting this was stupid. But, ultimately, there was no other way. And he was certain he wasn't being watched. He'd been careful to leave his phone at home. He'd had to hand it over when he'd been taken in for interviewing, and he could only assume it had been cloned, read or had some sort of bug put into it. Even if that hadn't happened, he was sure they could get GPS data from his network provider, or somehow else use his phone to track his movements. Either way, it was safer left at home.

He'd taken a circuitous route to where he was going. That way, even if anyone had seen him taking part of the journey, they wouldn't be able to deduce where he was going. This route was also much quieter, more secluded, and he'd soon know if someone was watching or following him. He'd not been daft enough to take his car, of course, and had walked the entire journey from his home.

Once he got there, he paused for a moment, looking

at the house. He knew the man had some money, but this was something else. He had to admit he'd wondered how much of that story had been true, given recent events. It had seemed a little odd that someone who'd won three million quid on the lottery would want to get a job in a factory because they got bored sitting at home, but he'd heard of similar things in the past. Either way, the guy had wanted a job. It didn't matter to Alistair whether he was a bored lottery winner or a fantasist. He could do the work, and that was all that mattered.

Of course, he was pleased to see he had been telling the truth, not least because it meant he really did have money. And money was what he was here for.

He squinted as he looked at the house, making sure there was no CCTV. He was surprised to see there wasn't. Even if there had been, he'd given himself two options: his coat had a hood to cover his face, and if push came to shove he was sure he could convince him to wipe the footage. Properly.

He walked along the long gravel driveway before reaching the house, then stepped up onto the large, half-moon-shaped front portico and rang the doorbell. After a short while, he saw movement through the frosted glass as the man came to answer the door.

'Alistair, hi. Everything okay?'

'Fine thanks. We need to talk. Can I come in?'

The man glanced behind him. 'Uh, yeah. No

problem. My wife's out, but she'll be back about ten-thirty.'

'That's fine,' Alistair said. 'This won't take long.'

The man led him through to the kitchen, where they sat at a large island counter in the middle of the room.

'So, what can I do for you?' he said.

'I think you probably know why I'm here,' Alistair replied.

'Well, I'm guessing it's to do with work. I heard all the stuff on the news earlier, and got the message we'd be closed for a couple of days. I presume they're doing tests and stuff?'

'Yes. They're swabbing all the machinery. Every corner of the factory. A whole team of them in there, going over everything meticulously.'

The man nodded slowly. 'Probably for the best. We need to find out what happened.'

'Yes,' Alistair said. 'Yes, we do. That's what I was hoping you might be able to help me with.'

The man's face remained unchanged. 'Me? How would I be able to help?'

'Come on. Don't take me for a fool. We both know what's been going on. I've seen your behaviour change recently. That day I caught you in the bottling room? It's all started making sense now.'

'Sorry, I don't know what you're trying to say, Alistair. I told you I was intrigued and wanted to see the new machinery. You said it was fine.'

'I know what you told me. And I know what I said. I also know why you were really in there. Now listen. This doesn't need to be a problem. I've had the CCTV from the factory floor wiped. It's gone.'

'So?'

'So there's no video evidence.'

The man cocked his head slightly. 'Of what? I presume you're trying to say you think I poisoned the juice somehow?'

'You tell me.'

'Either way, you're barking up the wrong tree. I know nothing about it.'

'Garden looks lovely,' Alistair said, nodding his head towards the enormous sliding glass doors on the long back wall of the kitchen. 'I like how you've done the lights.'

'Thank you.'

'I love the way it lights up those plants over there. Belladonna, aren't they?'

The man gave the briefest of pauses — just enough for Alistair to notice. 'They are,' he said. 'Didn't know you were a keen gardener.'

'I'm not,' Alistair replied, his voice level. 'But I've been doing a bit of reading. Deadly nightshade, they call them, don't they?'

'I believe so, yes.'

'You want to be careful not to eat the berries or the leaves. Highly toxic. That's where they get atropine from. You need quite a lot of it, mind, depending on the effect you're looking for. Do you have a lot of plants here?'

The man looked at him. 'Quite a few.'

Alistair nodded slowly. 'Yes. I imagine you do. Then again, you don't need me to tell you about atropine. What job was it you did before you won the lottery and took early retirement? Chemistry teacher, wasn't it?'

'What do you want, Alistair?'

'I want the same as you. I want all of this to go away. And we've both got something the other person wants, and which can make that happen.'

The man smiled and cocked his head slightly. 'Sorry, what do you think I want from you?'

'My silence. I don't need to know why you did it. Nor do I want to. But I need you to assure me it's finished and there's no chance of anyone else losing their life. I don't know how long the company can continue after this. In any case, there'll have to be redundancies. I want you to hand in your resignation beforehand.'

'I'm not entirely sure I'm following this, Alistair. You think I killed people, and rather than telling the police you chose to destroy CCTV footage from the factory. Why not tell them now? If you're that convinced it's me, tell them. But instead it's "hand in your notice and promise you won't kill anyone else". That doesn't make any sense.'

Alistair looked him in the eye. Despite the man's protestations, he knew he was standing face to face with the killer.

'It's the only hope I have of keeping the business alive and not losing everything. I'm not convinced there's much chance of that at all, but I panicked. As far as I see it, there's a way we can both come out of this relatively unscathed. A way that means I don't need to worry about the company collapsing, and you won't end up rotting in a prison cell for the rest of your life.'

The man looked at him and nodded. 'How much?'

'A million.'

Alistair didn't know what response he was expecting, but it certainly hadn't been laughter.

'A million quid? You must be joking.'

'You've got it. I know you have. From the lottery.'

'Alistair, you're standing in most of it. I don't know if you know how much this house cost.'

'Mortgage it.'

'What, is that before or after I resign from my job? Or are you suggesting I call a mortgage lender and ask them to give me a million quid, which I'll pay back through my minimum-wage hobby job at a juice factory that'll probably be bankrupt in a month?'

'It's not up to me how you get hold of it. That's your problem. I've protected you. I've put my neck on the line and risked a prison sentence for something that's kept the police off your back. If you don't want that to change, I'm going to need something back.'

Alistair watched as the man smiled back at him.

'You really don't get it, do you, Alistair?' He said. 'I didn't ask you to do any of that, so you've got absolutely no right to demand I pay for the privilege.'

'Alright. Have it your way. I'll tell the police everything.'

'Go ahead. Do you think I'm afraid of going to prison? Because I can tell you now I'm not.'

Alistair looked into the man's eyes, and what he saw worried him. He didn't know what it was — or why it was — but he clearly wasn't afraid of prison time. It was time for plan B. In for a penny, in for a pound.

'We've all got things we're afraid of,' Alistair said, taking a step forward. 'We've all got things we couldn't bear to lose. How old's your granddaughter now?'

The man's eyes narrowed as he registered the subtext in what Alistair was saying. He paused for a moment, and Alistair watched as the man's jaw tensed, his teeth grinding behind his lips. A few moments later, he spoke.

'I can do two-hundred-and-fifty-k by the weekend. The rest'll take me a couple of weeks. But that's it done, Alistair. No ifs, no buts.'

Alistair nodded and extended his hand. 'Done.'

33

Early the next morning, Caroline looked on as Dexter opened the team's morning briefing.

'The main development, I'm afraid, is that it looks as though we have a fourth victim,' he said, his face showing all the strain of an investigation that seemed to be running away from them. 'A seventy-six-year-old man from Uppingham, by the name of Jack Hayward. He had a number of health conditions, and lived independently, but his neighbour — a woman by the name of Veronica Cunningham — came in to check on him twice a day, as she left for work in the morning and when she returned at night. When she popped in yesterday evening, she found Jack dead in his chair. She called emergency services straight away, but he was unresponsive and declared dead at the scene. There was an almost-empty glass of juice on the table next to his chair, which Mrs Cunningham confirmed was Squeeze The Day grapefruit juice. We're trying to trace next of kin as we speak, but it seems he was never married and had no children. On the plus side, we've got a sample of the juice we've sent for further analysis. I'm expecting that, and the post-mortem, to show that the juice Jack drunk contained an extremely high dose of atropine. Any questions?'

Aidan put his hand up. 'I don't suppose we know of any links to the other three victims?'

Dexter shook his head. 'No, and I don't think we'll find one. This is random and indiscriminate, as far as I can tell. If the juice has been tampered with at the factory, there'd be no way of knowing who'd end up buying it and drinking it. Unfortunately, the victims are choosing themselves. The most worrying thing for me is that this implies the killer is doing it for reasons known only to them. For fun, even. It's not some form of targeted revenge or with any great motive other than to cause destruction. That makes them even more dangerous, and makes our job even harder.'

34

It was a good job work was closed, because he hadn't slept. He hadn't expected to. He knew he wouldn't sleep until this was all over, and there was only one way it could ever be considered over.

Either way, the outcome was likely to be the same. Avoiding prison was going to be almost impossible, but he'd always known that would be the case. His destiny was not his to control. He was at God's mercy.

Until the incident, the Lord had smiled kindly on him his whole life. He'd never wanted for anything, but still he'd received it. He'd lived his life in virtue, and for that he'd been rewarded. Until the incident.

It had been the ultimate test of his faith. Before it happened, his faith had been minimal, but existent. It was the sort of thing that would destroy anyone else's faith, but not his. With the Lord's help, he'd pulled through. And that had left him with an unwavering faith in the hand of God.

It was simple: it would only happen if it was deserved or meant to be. The Almighty wouldn't allow it if it wasn't for the greater good. Anything that God's nature allowed to happen was deserved. He supposed some people might think him soulless for having such an outlook on life, but it had never let him down. It stopped him from worrying about what might happen in the future. It was either right in God's eyes, or it wouldn't happen at all.

As he'd laid awake last night, he'd tried to console himself with that faith. Logically, it meant that Alistair Fletcher's threats meant nothing. God wouldn't allow it, and if He did it would be for good reason. But the difficulty came in determining what that reason was. Would He consider it a just punishment for killing those people? His instincts told him that if it required punishment, surely God wouldn't have allowed it in the first place? That had been his justification throughout: that the bottles could end up anywhere, in anybody's hands. They could even end up in the bin, or chucked down the sink. Anyone drinking them could die, could fall ill or could be fine. It wasn't his choice. The hand of God ruled all.

But what if God had allowed *that* act in the knowledge that his punishment would be far more just? That a handful of nobodies could be sacrificed in order to take his beautiful granddaughter? He hadn't considered that the Lord might have been taking a back seat in order to make things right later.

He'd always considered that his punishment would be prison. The Lord's redemption came in the strangest of ways, and he'd accept whatever He gave him. But that couldn't extend to Tamsin.

He hadn't anticipated that he might be dealing with pure evil in the form of Alistair Fletcher. He knew that evil was far more difficult to overcome. Although God's will was final, it was rarely immediate, unlike the threat to his granddaughter's life.

There was no other option. He was going to have to do something about it. This was his test. There was only one way out: Alistair Fletcher must die. He was well aware this fell outside the plan. It would require him to kill someone directly. The hand of God would be removed from play. It would no longer be down to fate; it would be entirely his doing. But it was justified, wasn't it? It was self-defence. He was defending his family against a direct and grave threat. He knew his God would understand him protecting a young child against the threat of pure evil.

Alistair Fletcher had proven himself a sinner. And for sinners, there was only one end.

35

Mark felt the warmth of the sun on his face as he squinted at his phone screen, the light glaring off the glass.

He was reading an article on Oakham Nub News, which he'd seen shared on Facebook. All of a sudden, things were starting to become clear.

RUTLAND POLICE ISSUE URGENT WARNING OVER 'DEATH' JUICE

Rutland Police have warned local residents to exercise 'extreme caution' after the discovery of a potentially deadly poison in bottles of locally-produced fruit juice.

The warning relates specifically to grapefruit juice made by Squeeze The Day, an organic juice manufacturer based just outside Oakham.

Detective Inspector Caroline Hills of Rutland Police said, "I implore everybody to take this very seriously indeed. If you are in possession of grapefruit juice produced by Squeeze The Day, please call the police non-emergency number on 101. If you have recently drunk any of this juice, please call NHS Direct on 111 for further advice. If you are experiencing any symptoms or ill effects, visit your nearest A&E department immediately, and if possible take the bottle with you."

As Mark read, the warmth from the sun was gradually replaced by a chill that crept up his spine and out through every nerve in his body.

He knew how these things worked. He'd picked up enough from what Caroline had told him over the years, and had learned to decode the subtleties in these sorts of statements. No deaths had been mentioned, but the language had been clear and stark. Although it had been worded to be taken seriously, but without causing undue panic by mentioning slow and painful deaths, Mark was left in no doubt this must be the case that had been plaguing Caroline.

His first thought was how guilty he felt. Although she'd asked him to trust her and told him the case was serious, he'd heard that so many times before. Of course, all of her cases were serious. If they weren't, CID wouldn't be working on them. And Caroline was right — there were families who needed justice, who'd lost loved ones and had the right to answers. He felt terrible that he'd put his need for family time above those for whom family time would never be the same again.

'Dad! Come and look at this!' Josh called from across the play area.

'There in a minute,' Mark replied, his voice barely louder than a mumble.

He scan-read the article again, trying to take in the implications. There must be bottles of this juice everywhere. He recognised the image accompanying the article — he'd seen their products for sale in local shops. If he remembered rightly, he'd even read something about them starting off on local market stalls a number of years ago. The article didn't say how many bottles had been affected, but it was safe to say it could potentially be thousands.

'Dad!'

'Yeah, I said give me a minute.'

Mark closed the web browser on his phone and opened his Contacts list. He scrolled down to Caroline's name and tapped *Call*.

36

It had been a long day, and Dexter was looking forward to getting home. They'd spent the day preparing for the Squeeze The Day staff interviews, and the investigation was now more or less a waiting game. The media campaign would, he hoped, minimise the chances of any further victims, and he knew it wouldn't be long before forensic evidence became apparent. They were close to rescuing the CCTV footage, too, and working on the assumption that Alistair Fletcher had wiped it to protect himself and the company, it seemed certain the killer was an employee of Squeeze The Day. That narrowed the list of suspects enormously. They'd already interviewed three, and planned to speak to the rest tomorrow.

His route out of Oakham along Braunston Road took him right past Alistair Fletcher's house. Although that had been merely a minor point of interest, tonight it took on a whole new significance.

As Dexter prepared to accelerate into the national speed limit zone at the very edge of town, he spotted something odd, but unmistakeable. It had been difficult to work out the detail in the dark, but it looked like the figure of a man quickly stepping into Fletcher's driveway and ducking behind the hedge.

Putting his car's brakes to the test, Dexter turned right into Glebe Way and parked up at the side of the road. Keeping his eye on Fletcher's house, he got out of his car and silently made his way back towards it.

He walked up the driveway, and was a few steps away from the door when he heard a noise to his right.

He turned his head and saw a man, who looked just as surprised to see him.

'Evening,' Dexter said. 'Sorry if I startled you. Is Alistair in?'

'Uh, I don't know,' the man replied, blinking heavily and clearing his throat. 'I don't think so. I came to see him too.'

Something didn't feel right to Dexter. The man looked vaguely familiar, but he couldn't place him. Then again, it wasn't unusual for a police officer in Rutland to have met people before.

'Can I ask who you are?' Dexter said.

'I work for Alistair, over at Squeeze The Day,' the

man replied. 'I wanted to see how he was after everything that's happened. Can't be easy for him.'

'That's very thoughtful of you, Mr…?'

'Truth be told, I was more worried about my own job. I wanted to know if it was safe or not. There's all sorts of rumours going round at the moment, and it's the sort of thing that gets you worried, you know?'

'I can imagine so. Sorry, sir. What is your name?' Dexter asked, growing increasingly impatient.

'Oh. Sorry,' the man replied. 'It's Fred.'

'Surname?'

'Barton.'

Even the man's name seemed familiar, Dexter thought. 'And what is it you do at Squeeze The Day, Mr Barton?'

The man shrugged. 'Whatever you want to call it, really. Factory floor.'

Dexter gave a smile. 'General dogsbody?'

'Something like that, yes.'

'You local?'

'Just over the other side of town. Stamford Road.'

Nice area, Dexter thought. *Expensive houses. Not the sort of place you'd expect to find a factory floor worker.*

'I'm heading back that way, as it happens. Can I give you a lift?'

'No, no I'm fine thanks,' Fred replied. 'Good to get the exercise.'

Dexter nodded slowly. 'Alright, Mr Barton. You take care.'

Dexter watched as the man headed off towards the main road. There were no signs of attempted entry at the property, but something felt very wrong.

Trying to dredge the depths of his memory, he took his phone out of his pocket and called Caroline.

37

'The name doesn't sound familiar,' Caroline said, as she held the phone to her ear with her shoulder, simultaneously attempting to stir a pan of pasta.

'Either way, that wasn't the weirdest bit,' Dexter replied at the other end of the phone. 'Why's a guy with a house like his doing factory work on minimum wage?'

'I don't know. Did you ask him? Maybe he's staying with family, or he might be renting a room.'

Dexter made a noise of disagreement. 'Nah, I don't think so. Call it intuition if you like, but there was something not right. The whole thing just seemed really suspicious. At first his story was that he was checking to see if Fletcher was alright, and then it was that he was worried about his job and wanted to find out what was going to happen. I mean, you send an email or make a phone call, don't you? You don't just pop round to the boss's house of an evening and start skulking around in his back garden.'

'True. Any previous to his name?'

'Not checked yet. That'll be the next step. Just thought I'd report back and let you know.'

'And Fletcher wasn't in?' Caroline asked.

'Nope. I did a thorough check of the property once Barton had gone. Nothing suspicious or out of place — just looks like he's not home.'

Caroline moved the pan off the hob and switched off the gas.

'Alright, Dex. I'll give Fletcher a call and check everything's okay. Last thing we need is him going AWOL, especially if he knows something.'

A few moments later, Caroline called Alistair Fletcher, who answered the phone after only two rings. At first, she thought he was drunk or had fallen asleep, but it soon dawned on her that he was merely distracted and somewhat sombre.

'Hello?' he slurred at the other end of the line.

'Mr Fletcher? It's DI Hills from Rutland Police. Is everything okay?'

'Mmmm. Yeah. What's up?'

'One of our officers popped by to see you at home. He said there was no sign of anybody in the house, so I wanted to check you were alright.'

A momentary pause — just enough for Caroline to notice.

'Oh. Yeah. Sorry. I'm not home. I'm at work, going over some papers.'

'I see. Anything important?'

There was a loud sigh at the other end of the phone. 'Yeah. I'm trying to work out how long we might have, and when I'm going to need to pull the plug and put the company into liquidation. Last thing we want is to not be able to pay people.'

'I'm sorry to hear that. How's it looking?'

'So so. Not ideal. Either way, I don't see how the company can continue if I'm likely to end up with a prison sentence.'

There was something in Fletcher's voice that sounded off. She couldn't be certain what it was, but she got the sense he hadn't resigned himself to bankruptcy and ruin in quite the way he made out.

Caroline wasn't sure whether it was an uneasy concern for Fletcher's welfare or a sense that he might be ready to talk, but she felt compelled to visit him. She was a big believer in face-to-face discussion, and it hadn't let her down yet. Was he ready to talk? Was there a plea bargain to be done? She didn't know, but she needed to find out.

'Sorry if this sounds a bit random,' she asked, 'but do you have a chap by the name of Fred Barton working for you?'

She could almost hear the intake of breath at the other end of the phone, although she didn't quite know what it meant.

'Yes. Why?'

'I was just wondering. When my colleague went to your house earlier, he found Mr Barton there. He said he'd come to see how you were doing, and to find out if his job was safe. I wondered if that struck you as normal or not.'

There was a momentary silence. 'I don't see anything wrong with it,' Fletcher answered, unconvincingly.

By now, Caroline was certain something was amiss.

'Would it be alright if I popped into the office on my way home?' she asked. 'There's a couple of things I'd like to go through with you.'

Fletcher sounded somewhat flustered. 'Uh, yes. That's fine. I've got a couple of jobs to get done first, though. How about I meet you at my house in an hour?'

Home territory, Caroline thought.

Fletcher detected the beat of silence. 'Or I can come to the station if that works better for you?'

'Alright,' Caroline said. 'I'll see you here in an hour.'

As she put the phone down and began to collect her thoughts, things started to fall into place.

38

Caroline looked at her watch. It had barely moved since she'd last looked at it. There were still forty-five minutes to go until she expected Fletcher.

As she paced her office and tried to organise her thoughts, there was a knock at the door. The ever-present Sara Henshaw entered, with a look on her face that bridged worry and delight.

'Guv, I think I've got something. You mentioned a Fred Barton earlier? The guy Dex found at Alistair Fletcher's house. I thought his name sounded familiar too, so I went back over the notes. I know why Dex recognised him. He was at All Saints Church the day Barbara Patchett died.'

Caroline felt a bolt of adrenaline surge through her. 'What? Are you sure?'

'Absolutely. He was there with his granddaughter.

Dex made a point of checking she was okay, because Barton was so visibly shocked by what'd happened. What are the odds that he works for the same factory that produced the grapefruit juice that killed her?'

Instinctively, Caroline knew the answer to that. *Consider every possibility*, she told herself. But as she did so, she only became more certain of the truth.

He hadn't meant to kill anybody specific. Certainly not anyone he knew. The death of Barbara Patchett, right in front of his eyes, had clearly shaken him. And a man who'd already indiscriminately killed four people was not someone she wanted shaken.

39

Although she'd recently experienced the drawbacks of having such a small team, Caroline was well aware that it had its advantages, too. The flexibility and can-do attitude of Rutland Police officers was something she needed to take advantage of right now, even if it had proved a major sticking point in her family life.

Even though she'd felt guilty calling Aidan on his way home, she had no doubt his response would be anything other than positive, and she'd been proven right.

'He might've already left,' she said, trying to speak as quickly but clearly as possible as Aidan listened on the other end of the phone. 'Either way, both Barton and Fletcher are trying to get to each other before the other one does, and it's not for a nice cosy chat.'

'You think they want each other dead?' Aidan asked.

'I do. That's why Barton went to find Fletcher and Dex found him skulking round the property. And the sense I got from speaking to Fletcher was that he knew what that meant, too, and needed to put a stop to it. They're both resigned to the fact the other must die. We've got uniform on their way to both Fletcher's and Barton's houses, but there are no more units available and by my reckoning you're the closest.'

'Very close as it happens,' Aidan replied, the *tick-tick-tick* of his car indicator providing a percussive backing track. 'I'm less than a minute away. I think I can see the building, but not sure which is which from here. I can see lights on the upper floor.'

Good, Caroline thought. If Fletcher hadn't left, there was every chance they could keep the two of them apart.

'Sounds like it might be the one. When I spoke to him, he said he was in the office. Let me know when you get close enough to confirm.'

'Yeah, I think it's the one,' Aidan said, somewhat distracted. 'Grab a pen, quick. PNC on Alpha Tango Seven Zero, Romeo Tango Golf. Repeat, Alpha Tango Seven Zero, Romeo Tango Golf. A maroon-coloured Jaguar.'

Caroline wrote the registration number down and passed it to Sara, who took it back to her computer.

'On it,' Caroline said to Aidan. 'What's the situation?'

'It's parked up down the road from Squeeze The Day. I've just watched a man get out of it. Difficult to tell his age because he's got a scarf over his mouth and nose, but I'd hazard a guess at mid to late sixties.'

'A scarf? In this weather?'

'That's what I thought,' Aidan replied. 'He's heading towards the factory building.'

'Where are you?'

'I turned right and parked up outside another unit, so I didn't spook him. Yep, definitely heading towards the building, and it's definitely Squeeze The Day. I can see the logo and the name on the front from here.'

'Registered to Frederick Edward Barton,' Sara shouted from her desk.

Caroline put her thumb up. 'PNC says the Jag's registered to Barton. It's him.'

'He's heading round the back. Shall I approach?' Aidan asked.

The sudden and unexpected judgement call hit Caroline hard. She knew what Barton had gone there to do, and she knew Fletcher was inside. But at the same time, both men were hell bent on murder and Aidan was unarmed. He didn't even have handcuffs.

Her instinct was to call Armed Response, but she quickly realised that wasn't an option. There was no way they'd get there in time from Leicester or Peterborough. But leaving Aidan to go in alone wasn't an option, either.

'Get closer to the building,' Caroline said, grabbing her car key from her bag. 'Don't approach him, but keep the building covered. Stay on the phone, and don't let him leave, but do not — repeat, do not — approach. I'm on my way.'

40

The roads were mercifully quiet, other than the roaring of the Volvo's engine as Caroline made quick progress towards Squeeze The Day. At the speed limit, the journey would usually take four or five minutes, but Caroline wasn't far off halving that.

The tyres skipped and squealed as she turned the corner into the industrial estate, her car losing as little speed as possible as it roared towards Squeeze The Day's premises. Her body lurched and she felt a twang in her neck as she stamped on the brake pedal and brought the Volvo to a sudden halt outside the building.

As she got out of the car, Aidan jogged over, having been keeping an eye on the building from a vantage point close by.

'Nothing yet,' he told her, as they looked up at the office windows, still lit from the inside, but with blinds obscuring their view of anything within. 'I've not heard anything either, but I don't know if that's good or bad.'

'Did you check out the rear of the building? If Barton's gone round there and not come back, there must be another entrance.'

'Not yet. You said not to approach, and I didn't know how tight it'd be behind there. I didn't want to get ambushed or take him unawares.'

'No. You did the right thing.'

Caroline and Aidan turned as they heard Dexter's car come to a screeching stop behind them.

'Dex,' Caroline said as her colleague got out of the car, 'With me. Aidan, keep an eye on the front of the building. Sara's had uniform redeployed from Barton's house, and they're on their way over. They must have missed him by minutes. They'll be here any second.'

'Shouldn't we wait for them?' Dexter asked. 'We don't know if either of them's armed.'

'We don't have the luxury of waiting,' Caroline replied. 'The one thing we do know is they're both inside that building right now, and both hell bent on making sure the other is dead. We're going in.'

Dexter didn't argue. There wasn't time, and there was certainly no point. He watched as Caroline ran off towards the back of the building, and quickly followed.

41

Fred wondered how daft Alistair Fletcher really thought he was. He must have felt so clever, getting that copper over to his house to try and catch Fred in the act. He'd known Fred would go straight to the factory to find him, too. But Alistair had taken that cockiness a little too far, as per usual.

Leaving the office lights on had been smart, to a point. It had been the invitation to enter. But he'd gone too far in leaving the fire door not only unlocked, but ajar. That was when it had all fallen into place in Fred's mind. It was a trap.

It had been too obvious, though. Far too obvious. Alistair had over-played his hand, gone one step too far, and that would be his downfall. Fred would make sure of it.

The cleaning cupboard was dark — pitch black —

but that was fine. With the door open just a crack, it gave him a great view towards the stairs that led up to the offices. He knew what Alistair had expected. How he'd thought he was one step ahead, when really he was two behind. With CCTV covering the front entrance, he'd known Fred would try to get in through the back. Once inside, he could make it as far as the corridor upstairs before CCTV would pick him up again. But he wasn't going to make it that far.

Fred knew Alistair would be watching. Remotely, perhaps. He'd have seen him go round the back of the building. And he'd be waiting, sitting up in that little office of his, expecting a knock at the door at any moment. He was probably hiding behind the door with a weapon, ready to take Fred by surprise. What a fool! The surprise would be all his.

As a smirk began to break across his face, Fred heard footsteps. At first, he wondered if it was Alistair coming down the stairs to find out why Fred hadn't come up, which was precisely what he'd hoped would happen. And when he did, Fred would jump out and knock him to the floor, before putting the nylon noose over his head and pulling tight. Alistair wouldn't stand a chance.

But the noise wasn't coming from the stairs. It was coming from outside. Oh, that was even better! Alistair had thought he was even cleverer, second-guessing that Fred would have anticipated the ambush, and had hidden outside, so he could follow him in and take *him* by surprise! A triple bluff. It was beautiful. Almost admirable.

He held his breath as the footsteps came closer, shadows moving across the floor.

Shadows.

Not one. Two.

He lifted his eyes, and realised immediately who they were. Coppers. He recognised the black one from Alistair's house. He wanted to laugh, realising that Alistair had done him again. He wasn't going to ambush Fred himself — he'd laid a trap for him and sent the police in to nab him themselves. He should've known. Should've guessed. It wasn't as if Alistair Fletcher was ever going to get his own hands dirty. Not if he could get some other poor sap to do the work for him.

The joke was on him, though. Even though he'd expected Fred to have come bounding up the stairs to his office, he hadn't even considered the possibility that Fred would be hiding downstairs, just feet from the fire exit.

Never mind. Fred would just have to sit it out and wait for the police to leave, and then he would hunt Fletcher down for himself.

As he wondered to himself whether his employer was even in the building, or whether he'd been hiding out somewhere else, he heard raised voices from upstairs. That answered that question, he thought, but why were they shouting?

He listened more closely, and realised he couldn't hear Alistair. It was the coppers who were shouting, their voices getting louder as they made their way back along the upstairs corridor.

They were coming his way. In a couple of seconds they'd appear in view — and, potentially, he in theirs.

He reached up to the coat hook and pulled the door towards him, shuffling a little further back into the cleaning cupboard, although there was barely any room to do so.

As he tucked in his stomach and pulled himself further in, he felt the side of the plastic racking behind him suddenly give way with a small snap. It didn't have room to collapse or fall apart, but Fred's heart lurched as the extra inch it created meant he'd inadvertently pulled the door completely shut.

He held his breath. The coppers must have heard. They must have. To him, it sounded like a gunshot going off, but he wasn't sure how close they were at the time.

A couple of seconds later, he heard them pass the door and leave the building even more quickly than they'd come in. And with their voices now more clearly audible, he heard exactly what they were saying.

42

'Dex, get your car out of the way! Aidan, call the fire service. Now!'

Caroline threw open the door of her Volvo, started the engine, pushed it into reverse and floored it. With the car far enough away to be safe, she switched off the engine again and got out. As she did so, the uniformed officers who'd been at Fred Barton's house arrived on the scene.

'Keep back!' she yelled. 'The building's on fire. There's flames and smoke pouring out of the rooms upstairs. It's already too far out of control for us to handle ourselves. The fire service is on the way.'

'Is anyone in there?' one of the officers shouted.

'We don't know. We don't think so, but we couldn't get very far. The fire was about halfway along the corridor. We kicked a couple of doors open and couldn't see anyone, but it was spreading so quickly, and we couldn't get any further. We had to get out.'

Caroline looked at her watch. The fire station wasn't much further from here than the police station, and she'd made it in a few minutes. She prayed they wouldn't be long, and that if anyone was inside, they'd be able to get the fire under control quickly enough to save them.

But as she looked back at the building and saw thick black smoke enveloping the windows and billowing out through the air vents, she knew that was going to be highly unlikely.

43

Fred fumbled in the darkness, desperately clamouring for the door handle he quickly realised didn't exist.

Of course it didn't, he thought. Who would put a door handle on the *inside* of a cupboard?

He pushed against the door as much as he could, which wasn't a lot. Without any space behind him, he couldn't build up enough force to break the latch. All he could do was lean against it and hope, but it soon became clear hope wouldn't be enough.

He pulled his hands back the few inches he could, hammering his hands against the door and yelling for help, fighting for volume over the piercing bell of the fire alarm. He knew the police wouldn't be able to hear him. They would have got well back, keeping themselves safe while they waited for the fire brigade.

All he could do was to keep shouting, hoping the first firemen on the scene would hear him and rescue him.

As he took another deep breath for yet another round of yelling for help, he felt the first wisps of acrid smoke hit the back of his throat. Bitter. Choking. Apt, he thought.

He kept trying to shout, but each lungful of air he took got thicker and heavier with smoke.

He heard cracking and splintering. It sounded close by.

If he thought about it carefully, he could convince himself his stomach and groin were growing increasingly warm.

Within seconds, he realised he didn't need much convincing.

By now, the barely noticeable warmth had grown into a searing heat that began to make his clothes smoulder.

As the smoke from his jeans and jumper mingled with the thick fumes from the other side of the door, the pain became too intense to be bearable. As speckled stars began to dance in front of his eyes, the smell was joined by that of his own burning flesh.

44

The immediate aftermath of a murder investigation was always a time of discovery. Even when the killer's identity and motives had been known already, there was still a huge amount to be learned through the interview process and court proceedings.

Like most detectives, Caroline wasn't happy merely identifying and arresting the guilty party. For justice to truly be done, lessons had to be learned. It was a difficult realisation to accept that anyone could learn lessons from a murderer, but when her job was to not only catch criminals but help prevent crime happening in the first place, she knew there was no-one better to learn from than the criminals themselves.

If nothing else, it was a fascinating insight into the mind of a person who could so easily and indiscriminately snuff out the life of a fellow human being. And even when murder happened on the spur of the moment, or an otherwise normal person snapped and crossed a line they never thought they would, that provided an even more fascinating insight as far as Caroline was concerned. The thought that any one of us could find ourselves in that situation — waking up one perfectly normal morning and ending the day a murderer — was something that entranced and mesmerised her.

In the case of Fred Barton, she wouldn't get the chance to look him in the eye and hear it spoken in his own words. She couldn't lie — there was a huge part of her that revelled in the knowledge that he'd died a slow and excruciating death. She'd lain awake for hours overnight, trying to decide whether she was pleased Barton had used such a high dose of atropine that his victims had died quickly and without prolonged agony, or whether a much lower dose would have given them a chance of realising what it was and saving more lives.

From what she'd read about atropine, it was rare for it to kill so quickly. The enormous doses Barton had used meant there had been virtually no hope of survival. For most — if not all — of his victims, death would have come before many of the classic symptoms had even had a chance to present themselves. The effects on their heart and lungs would have been irreversible without immediate medical treatment. The huge dose meant that could never have been immediate enough.

The team had received a number of reports from members of the public who believed they'd ingested poisoned juice. There were, of course, the usual crank calls from people who'd drunk the juice and fancied their chances of a big payday, as well as the terminally panicked who were convinced this must be the cause of their persistent headaches or gammy toe. But amongst the dross were a small handful of reports that were worth looking at more closely. Three in particular reported having drunk a small amount of juice, but found it far too bitter and unpalatable and chucked the rest down the sink. They'd all been ill since, with symptoms that closely mirrored classic atropine poisoning, but had made full recoveries. It was regrettable they hadn't sought medical help at any point, but then none of them had drawn the link between drinking the juice and feeling ill a few hours later. Having only consumed one or two small mouthfuls each, they'd been fortunate to ingest only a small dose — little enough for it not to kill them. Nevertheless, the police had arranged for them all to undergo a full medical examination to make sure no long-term damage had been done.

So far as they could tell, Barton's antics had resulted in only the four deaths they knew about. The public messaging campaign and the concerted effort to recall

all remaining bottles had been a success, and with every day that passed it seemed the odds of the list growing longer than four diminished.

In any case, it seemed Barton had been hell-bent on killing his victims, despite them selecting themselves at random. Rather than introducing atropine at the juicing stage, it had been done at bottling, with the bottles picked entirely at random. He couldn't have known who would ultimately buy and drink each bottle, but he'd already decided they must die. This hadn't been someone messing around or not knowing what effect their actions would have. Despite its randomness, it had been deliberate, calculated and pre-planned.

The motives behind that fascinated Caroline, and she'd been intrigued to have been put in touch with Dawn Godsall, a clinical psychologist and psychotherapist Fred Barton had been a client of for some time. Although medical professionals and therapists were usually bound by confidentiality, that became void when there were clear and present dangers to human life.

Caroline pulled up outside Dawn Godsall's house in Lyndon and switched off her car's engine. No wonder she asked her clients to visit her here, Caroline thought. The surroundings seemed ideal for relaxing and opening the mind. And when it came to minds, she could only wonder at what she might discover inside Fred Barton's.

'Thank you for seeing me on a Saturday,' Caroline said. 'I noticed you don't work weekends.'

'Exactly,' Dawn replied, smiling. 'It has the added bonus that I didn't need to cancel any clients.'

Dawn seemed friendly and amiable — precisely the sort of person anyone would feel comfortable opening up to, which she presumed was the whole point. Once the coffee had been made, they sat down at Dawn's kitchen table.

'I wasn't quite sure where was best to do this,' she said. 'I'd usually take you through to my therapy room because it's work-related, but it somehow seems a little odd having you "on the couch", so to speak, considering the circumstances.'

'Here's just fine,' Caroline said. 'Do you actually have a couch?'

Dawn let out a small titter. 'No, I'm afraid not, despite what Hollywood would have you believe.'

Caroline smiled. Although she herself had spent time in counselling, that had been her only real experience of the practice and it was impossible to know if that was representative of the whole.

'First of all, I wanted to say thank you for speaking with me today,' Caroline said. 'I know it must have come as a shock to find out what had happened.'

Dawn gave a heavy sigh. 'You can say that again. Believe me, if I had any inkling Fred was capable of anything like this, or any suspicion whatsoever, I would have reported it.'

'I know. Don't worry, you're not under any suspicion or anything like that. We just want to find out more about what made Fred Barton tick. See if we can unravel any threads and provide some sort of closure or background as to why he did what he did.'

'Okay,' Dawn replied. 'Well, I guess I should start at the beginning. Fred started coming to see me about eight months ago, following the death of his daughter. He'd been holding it together for the rest of his family, but the cracks had been starting to show and behind closed doors he was falling apart. Those are his words, not mine. It seemed to be a classic case of burying emotions and refusing to deal directly with traumatic experiences. There's a certain type of people — perhaps a generation — who've been brought up to bury difficult situations and get on with life. Stiff upper lip, don't let it get to you, all that sort of thing. Of course, we now know that approach doesn't work, and actually causes damaging and often irreversible changes to the brain and its thought processes, which often manifest themselves in seemingly unconnected ways. Ultimately, the brain *has* to process these emotions and experiences. When we don't give it the space and procedure to do that, it tries to do it in other ways. One basic example of that is how phobias develop, or why particular situations or events can be hugely traumatic triggers for people, even though they might not realise why.'

'So was this a little while after his daughter's death?' Caroline asked.

'Yes, almost a year after. He knew that was what he was struggling with, and understandably so. He told me he'd been having some dark and unusual thoughts, which he recognised might have been his brain's way of trying to deal with the trauma.'

Caroline's eyebrows rose slightly. 'What sort of dark and unusual thoughts?'

'It was mostly to do with trying to justify what had happened, or apportion blame. Almost a sort of inner anger, but not directed at anything in particular. From a clinical point of view, he hadn't given himself the time to deal with the natural process of death and grieving, and whenever his mind had the space to do so, it was almost as if the shock hit him all over again. He spoke a lot about religion, particularly as the sessions went on. I thought at first maybe it just wasn't a subject he thought was relevant or important to bring up at first, but it soon became apparent it was something that was growing for him. He hadn't been a lifelong churchgoer, or anything like that, but he seemed to have become fascinated with God's will, as he put it. Part of his way of dealing with the grief and trauma was to somehow rationalise it. It's very difficult to apportion blame to cancer, particularly when you feel there needs to be a cause behind *that*.

'He'd been starting to build this theory that God had somehow chosen for his daughter to die. He said he didn't know why, but he believed there had to be a reason, and that because he believed in a benevolent and omnipotent God, that ultimately that reason must have been good and virtuous, despite appearing otherwise. Psychologically speaking, it's one of the things that lead people to say someone has been "chosen by God" or "joined the angels" when they die. It justifies a seemingly meaningless and desperately sad event by reframing it positively.'

'Like a sort of sacrifice?' Caroline asked.

'I suppose so, yes. Maybe martyrdom might be a better way of putting it. A lot of religious folk tie it back in with Jesus having given the ultimate sacrifice of his life and become a martyr. Like I say, unresolved trauma and grief can come out in some very odd ways.'

'And was this something he'd talked about recently?'

Dawn nodded. 'Oh yes. The concept of God's will and the rationalisation of chance events seemed to become a dominant theme. It's strange, because in our early sessions we seemed to be making so much progress in helping him deal with his grief. I thought he was making great strides, but then he seemed to knock himself off course somewhat.'

'What do you think caused that?' Caroline asked.

'It's difficult to say. We never did get to the bottom of it. Sometimes, when people see a therapist for the first time they tend to clam up and say the right things, or perhaps steer the conversation in a certain way or towards topics they want to address rather than ones they need to address. As a therapist, we have to trust that what the person is telling us is true. There are exceptions, but on the whole, if someone displays signs of improvement and claims to be seeing real benefits from therapy, we have no reason to disbelieve that.'

'Was it the mentions of religion and God's will that made you wonder?'

Dawn nodded again. 'It was. We'd done a lot of work on talking about illness, about the huge percentage of people who develop terminal illnesses, how death is something that comes to us all eventually and that we can choose to focus on the decades of happy times rather than those final moments. He seemed to be making real progress, but I think things had been continuing to brew in the background. He wasn't the sort of person who opened up easily. Although I thought he'd begun to do so, in retrospect I think he was just saying the right things. Of course, by the time we got to that point, he'd felt comfortable enough in my presence that he inevitably started to open up these real thoughts and theories.'

Caroline thought about this for a few moments. 'Look, I know you had no suspicions Fred was capable of anything like this, but in your professional opinion, and knowing him in the way you did, what do you think caused him to do what he did? Why kill people? And so randomly, too. It doesn't seem to make any sense.'

Dawn let out a long sigh. 'It's very difficult to say. The brain's a complex thing, and I'm sure in the fullness of time the details will start to fill themselves in. The only person who could answer those questions is Fred, and he's no longer with us. But if you want my personal opinion…?'

Caroline nodded.

'I'd put it down to his borderline obsession with God's will. Because he'd used it to rationalise his daughter's death, the belief had to be incredibly strong. Unshakeable, in fact. If there was any doubt on that front, ultimately it meant his daughter's death had been unnecessary and unjustified. I…' Dawn stopped, taking a moment to compose herself. 'I wonder if I might have been indirectly responsible myself.'

Caroline cocked her head. 'You? How?'

'When Fred started to talk about God's will, and how he used that to explain his daughter dying so young, I tried to steer him away from it. I didn't believe it was healthy to shy away from the facts, or to use religion as a sticking plaster. After all, he came to me because he hadn't processed the trauma properly, and I didn't feel this approach was going to be any more helpful.'

'You can't blame yourself for that.'

'I know. And I know hindsight is a wonderful thing,

but even us therapists aren't immune from self-doubt. In recent weeks, he started talking more in-depth about how God's will could absolve guilt. I didn't know what he meant by it. On a subconscious level, I mean. I thought maybe he was just expanding on the topic, developing his theory. I tried to steer him back towards a healthier approach, but he kept talking about it. And then he started to ask me my thoughts on it.'

Dawn fell silent.

'Go on,' Caroline whispered.

'He asked me how much I believed chance played a role in people's fate. He used the example of someone cutting the brake lines on another person's car. He suggested that they were only setting up the possibility of a tragedy, and that ultimately it was up to God's will as to whether the other person got into the car, whether they drove it, whether a warning light came on, whether they drove too fast, went down a hill, chose a busy route. And I remember him specifically asking, if his theory was true and that God's will was real, who was responsible in that situation.'

'And what did you say?'

Dawn looked at her, her eyes glassy with approaching tears.

'I said I didn't know.'

45

Caroline wasn't relishing the thought of another meeting with Chief Superintendent Derek Arnold, but she reluctantly had to accept it was needed. If nothing else, she'd have a story to tell the grandchildren: that she'd personally witnessed a Chief Superintendent's presence in the office on a weekend.

As at the conclusion of any major case, there were lessons to be learned, and she hoped one of those would be that Rutland needed a better staffed and resourced Major Crimes unit.

She knew it was an almost impossible ask. After all, protocol was that anything much more serious than basic rural crime was passed on to the East Midlands Special Operations Unit, who existed to deal with precisely these sorts of investigations. Regardless, breaking with protocol hadn't done them any harm over the past year or two, and Caroline felt empowered to stand her ground and fight the corner of her small yet impressive team.

She'd already anticipated how the powers-that-be would spin things. If she pointed out how under-staffed and under-resourced they were, the answer would be that this was why EMSOU existed, and that county forces weren't designed to handle major crimes. But if she defended this by pointing out how successful her small county team had been in solving large cases, they'd use that to prove their point that Rutland was perfectly adequately staffed and resourced, because if it wasn't, they wouldn't have succeeded in them.

The approach had to be subtle, but firm. She needed to make it clear that, yes, the team had been successful in the cases it'd taken on, but only just, and that it was now becoming unsustainable. Although she knew the response and proposed solution would involve protocol and EMSOU, she had her own reply to that.

In the time she'd been living and working in Rutland, she'd seen how small communities operated. She'd had first-hand experience as to how a local approach and local knowledge went so much further than drafting in the heavy boots from Leicester, Derby or Nottingham. Yes, it might have been unconventional. It may well have gone against protocol, unwritten or otherwise. But it worked. And when it came to communities like these, there was a very strong argument it was the best approach possible.

Her days in the Met had shown her how working closely with communities could prove invaluable when it came to solving crimes. They'd made great strides in breaking down inner-city gang culture in London — something which had seemed insurmountable only a few years earlier — through bringing the disaffected and lucky escapees into their own ranks, bridging the collossal gap of understanding between street gangs and the police. It was a far cry from Rutland in so many ways, but the same core belief applied: that doing away with the 'us and them' approach and replacing it with real community relations, dialogue and understanding brought lasting results.

She sat down opposite Arnold and waited for him to steer the conversation. As she'd predicted, he was keen to offer his thoughts and feelings on Operation Kayak, although they were — as always — without much substance.

'Some might say it was a stroke of luck,' he offered, talking about the night of the fire.

'I'm not sure luck had much to do with it, if anything, sir. On the contrary, it was DS Antoine's instincts that led him to believe something wasn't quite right about Fred Barton, and it was DC Henshaw's eagle eye that joined the dots. And that's not even mentioning my own quick recognition of what was going on, and how both Fred Barton and Alistair Fletcher were hell-bent on wiping each other out to protect themselves.'

'I was more meaning that it was lucky he got trapped in that cleaning cupboard. You and DS Antoine jogged straight past him without even spotting him. Twice. You're lucky he wasn't able to get out, else he'd be well away by now.'

Caroline didn't respond. She still wasn't entirely sure herself whether it was better Fred Barton was dead or if there'd have been any advantage to anyone if he'd had his day in court.

Arnold continued. 'What's the latest on Fletcher? Still progressing?'

'Nothing much new,' Caroline replied. 'He admitted to arson in his first interview after the fire. We're preparing everything for the CPS, and he's on bail pending further inquiries.'

'He'll be looking at quite a stretch.'

'Potentially. He'll have a decent chance of claiming some level of coercion in covering up the CCTV, especially now there are police records showing Barton had paid him a visit at home and that there was some level of threat towards Fletcher.'

'Only after the fact, though, surely?'

'True, but it's enough to plant the seed in a judge's mind that the threat might've been present before that.

And, of course, we don't have Barton's testimony to prove otherwise. Either way, I think it's likely his defence will come up with some pretty convincing mitigating circumstances for the arson. There's the financial situation and pressures, the immediate threat to his life and the possibility of him arguing some level of self-defence. And the link with the coercion he might claim, of course.'

'Of course. But I think self-defence might be pushing it a bit much. You don't lure someone into a factory then burn the place down in self-defence.'

'No, but I think it'd be unwise not to prepare ourselves for that being a possible argument his team will put forward. One step ahead and all that.'

Arnold nodded. 'Very wise. Well, keep me updated. You've done us proud again, Caroline. You've got a fantastic team there. I'm consistently amazed at the results you get. We all are.'

Caroline pursed her lips. It wasn't like Arnold to blow smoke up her backside, and there was a reason he hadn't mentioned her request for extra resources. She suspected this was his attempt to sweeten her, as well as pointing out just how well the team was doing already, smoothing the way for him to sweep her request under the carpet.

'Thank you, sir,' she said. 'But as I mentioned to you recently, it really isn't sustainable in any way. I know how it might look on paper, but as the one on the ground who manages the team from day to day, I really can't stress my concerns strongly enough.'

Arnold looked at her for a moment, then slowly nodded. 'I know. You said. And I put your case to the powers that be, I can promise you. I fought your corner very hard. And they fought back, as the people with the purse strings tend to do. Like you said yourself, all seems perfectly fine on paper, and paper's all they think about.'

Caroline clenched her jaw. She knew she'd be facing an uphill battle, but to be shut down so completely at just the moment she'd risked losing everything was unforgivable. She thought of Dexter, Sara and Aidan and the extraordinary hours and commitment they put in. She thought of Mark and her boys and everything they'd put up with. The sacrifices they'd all made. The relationships she'd put at risk.

'Sir, I —'

'Ultimately, though, I think the decision they made was fair.'

'Sir—'

'How does one extra permanent team member, plus rapid deployment of support staff on major incidents sound?'

Caroline sat, silent and stunned.

'Sorry?'

'I know one doesn't sound a lot, but it's a twenty-five percent increase on your permanent staffing numbers. The rapid deployment aspect will take a bit of working out, but they're confident it can be done. It'll mean much faster access to support staff if and when major incidents arise in the future. Provided we're not too thinly stretched elsewhere, of course. They're even talking about negotiating secondments from EMSOU.'

Caroline felt her eyebrows rise towards the top of her head. 'Right. Well, I don't know what to say, sir. Thank you, I guess.'

'That'd be a good start,' Arnold replied, smiling. 'I'll keep you updated on the process. But believe me, I'll be pushing them on it. You know what these people are like. If they can drag their heels, they bloody well will. Now it's been promised, I'm going to make sure it happens.'

Caroline felt a beaming smile appearing on her face for the first time in many days.

46

It felt strange sitting in her own house, waiting for the rest of her family to return from holiday. Although things had been smoothed over with Mark, she knew she'd have work to do in order to rebuild things properly.

The meeting with Arnold had been a huge help. Although Mark had been dismissive of her chances of securing extra resources and reducing the impact of work on her home life, she could now show him that was all about to change — and this time for the better.

She watched as Mark's hire car pulled onto the driveway, before it came to a halt and the headlights switched off. With a smile on her face, she went to the front door, opened it and ran towards her sons with open arms.

'Mum!'

'Hello, sweethearts. God I've missed you. Did you have a nice time?'

'Yeah!' Archie yelled, mere inches from her ear. 'Yesterday we went in the rock pools and Dad caught a massive crab!'

'Wow, that sounds fun! How big was it?'

'Like this big!' Archie replied, holding his arms as far apart as he could. 'And then he ate it for dinner!'

'Obviously he didn't,' Josh said, with the attitude and tone of a child a good few years older. 'He had crab, but obviously not *that* crab. We *literally* watched him put it back in the water.'

'It might have been the same crab. You never know.'

'It obviously wasn't.'

'You don't know that.'

'I know you're an idiot.'

'Alright boys, that's enough,' Caroline said, putting out a placating hand towards them. 'I know you've had a long journey and you're tired from having so much fun, so why don't we all go inside and order a pizza?'

'God, I thought you'd never ask,' Mark said, appearing from behind the car with armfuls of luggage. 'I got a cheese toastie in a service station just outside Cambridge. I had two mouthfuls before my body started screaming for mercy. Give me a hand with these, will you? Driving this bloody hire car's knackered my back.'

Caroline grabbed a couple of bags from him, noting

the boys had already gone inside the house without carrying anything more than their own weight.

'How was the journey?' she asked.

'Put it this way. The cheese toastie was the highlight.'

'Oh dear. That bad?'

'Next time I suggest a break, promise me we're getting on a plane. They tend not to get stuck in tailbacks on the A14.'

Caroline smiled. 'Good news on the work front, though,' she said, hoping to cheer him up a little — although she could tell his cantankerous act was a poor cover for how pleased he was to see her. 'The Chief Super managed to get what we wanted. A twenty-five percent increase on the team's permanent staff numbers and rapid access to support staff during major incidents.'

'Twenty-five percent?' Mark replied as they reached the front door. 'Isn't that one person?'

'I'm not complaining. One person can make a huge difference. Either way, it'll stop work impacting on our home life as much. It's definitely a good thing.'

Caroline closed the door behind them as Archie's ear-piercing screech reverberated off the walls, threatening to burst her eardrums.

'Get *off* it! It's mine!'

'Welcome home,' she said, with a small chuckle.

'Thanks,' Mark replied. 'I'll leave you to sort that one out. I think it's safe to say it's your turn.'

'I think that's fair. In that case, mine's a double pepperoni stuffed crust.'

'On it. Anything else you want?'

Caroline stopped halfway up the stairs and looked back at him.

'How about a holiday?'

WANT MORE?

I hope you enjoyed *Kiss of Death*.

If you want to be the first to hear about new books — and get a couple of free short stories in the meantime — head to:

adamcroft.net/vip-club

Two free short stories will be sent to you straight away, and you'll be the first to hear about new releases.

For more information, visit my website: **adamcroft.net**

ACKNOWLEDGEMENTS

As is always the case, you and I have a number of people to thank and blame for the existence of this book.

The entire concept would've been impossible were it not for the generous input of Dr Kathryn Harkup, whose self-appointed job title is 'science communicator, chemist and vampirologist'. As much as I wanted to ask daft questions about Dracula, I instead asked her even dafter ones about poisons, about which she is also very much an expert. All in all, I'd advise people not to mess with her. If she starts getting into guns or nuclear weapons, we know something's up.

On the off-chance she doesn't intend to overthrow civilisation, I heartily recommend you buy a copy of her book *A Is for Arsenic: The Poisons of Agatha Christie*. And even if she does, at least you'll have read a jolly good book prior to the apocalypse.

Where my fictional portrayals of atropine poisoning are accurate, all credit must go to Kathryn. Where I've stretched science a little, I take full responsibility. I wouldn't dare do anything else when pitted against an expert in vampires and poisons.

Thank you to Graham Bartlett, former Chief Superintendent and City Commander of Brighton & Hove Police for answering my endless daft questions about police procedure, post mortem and toxicology, and helping me to make my books as accurate as possible on that front.

To Lucy, Bev, Jo and my mum for casting their eyes over early versions of the book and pointing out all the rubbish bits. I think I changed most of them.

To Nick Castle for another fantastic cover design. He also gets my apologies for being a fusspot and needing him to send twenty alternative cover designs before I ultimately and inevitably decide his initial one was best anyway.

Huge thanks also go to Covid-19, which struck the Croft household in February 2022. As I was fortunate enough to be asymptomatic, it gave me the perfect opportunity to lock myself in my office for a week, away from my family whingeing endlessly about 'chest pain' and 'agony', so I could finish the book. Honestly, I don't know what all the fuss was about.

To you, the reader, for buying this book, which I must admit is pretty handy and does make my life easier. This whole exercise would be a bit weird otherwise.

And of those readers, extra special thanks go to my

Patreon supporters. But more about them over the page…

A SPECIAL THANK YOU TO MY PATRONS

Thank you to everyone who's a member of my Patreon program. Active supporters get a number of benefits, including the chance of having a character named after them in my books. In this book, Dawn Godsall and PC Daniel MacLagan were named after Patreon supporters.

With that, I'd like to give my biggest thanks to my small but growing group of Patreon supporters: Alexier Mayes, Andy Jeens, Angela Pepper, Ann Sidey, Anne Davies, Barbara Tallis, Brian Savory, Carla Powell, Cheryl Hill, Claire Blincoe, Claire Evans, Daniel MacLagan, Dawn Godsall, Dawn Philip, Emiliana Anna Perrone, Estelle Golding, Francis W Markus, Gordon Aldred, Gordon Bonser, Helen Brown, Helen Weir, Ian Harding, Jay Vernalls, Jean Wright, Jeanette Moss, Jenny Mustoe, Jo Goodliffe, Josephine Graham, Julie Devonald Cornelius, Karina Gallagher, Ken Mounser, Kerry Hammond, Kerry Robb, Kirstin Anya Wallace, Leigh Hansen, Lesley Somerville, Linda Anderson, Lisa Bayliss, Lisa Lewkowicz, Lisa-marie Thompson, Lynne Davis, Lynne Lester-George, Mandy

Davies, Mark and Julie, Mary Fortey, Maureen Hutchings, Mrs J Budnik-Hillier, Nigel M Gibbs, Paul Wardle, Paula Holland, Peter Tottman, Rachel, Ruralbob, Sally Catling, Sally-Anne Coton, Sam, Samantha Harris, Sarah Hughes, Sean Halliday, Sharon Oakes, Sheanne Lovatt, Sim Croft, Sue, Susan Bingham, Susan Cox, Susan Fiddes, Sylvia Crampin, Tracey Clark, Tremayne Alflatt and Vickie Hughes. You're all absolute superstars.

If you're interested in becoming a patron, please head over to patreon.com/adamcroft. Your support is hugely appreciated.

SIMON COLE QPM

Just as we were preparing to send this book to print, I learned the sad news that Simon Cole QPM, former Chief Constable of Leicestershire Police, had passed away at the age of 55.

Simon had retired from his role just twelve days earlier, and had been an enormous help and encouragement to me over the past two years.

A Leicestershire boy all his life, Simon was awarded the Sir Robert Peel Medal by the Institute of Criminology at Cambridge University — an award given each year for Outstanding Leadership in Evidence Based Policing. In 2014, he was awarded the Queen's Police Medal in the 2014 New Year's Honours List, which allowed him use of those rather funky letters after his name.

Despite having a BA (Hons) in English Literature, he

was a keen supporter of my work and was often willing to tweet and retweet about the series on Twitter, always without being asked.

The dénouement of *In Cold Blood* wouldn't have been possible without his insight and assistance on the inner workings of ANPR and intel-driven roads policing, and I'm certain the book's ending would've been weaker were it not for Simon's invaluable input.

He will be sorely missed not only by his family and friends, but by the entire policing community and everyone he impacted with his amiable help and generosity.

HAVE YOU LISTENED TO THE RUTLAND AUDIOBOOKS?

The Rutland crime series is now available in audiobook format, narrated by Leicester-born **Andy Nyman** (Peaky Blinders, Unforgotten, Star Wars).

The series is available from all good audiobook retailers and libraries now, published by W.F. Howes on their QUEST and Clipper imprints.

W.F. Howes are one of the world's largest audiobook publishers and have been based in Leicestershire since their inception.

W.F. HOWES LTD

QUEST

ADAM CROFT

With over two million books sold to date, Adam Croft is one of the most successful independently published authors in the world, having sold books in over 120 different countries.

In February 2017, Amazon's overall Author Rankings briefly placed Adam as the most widely read author in the world at that moment in time, with J.K. Rowling in second place. And he still bangs on about it.

Adam is considered to be one of the world's leading experts on independent publishing and has been featured on BBC television, *BBC Radio 4*, *BBC Radio 5 Live*, the *BBC World Service*, *The Guardian*, *The Huffington Post*, *The Bookseller* and a number of other news and media outlets.

In March 2018, Adam was conferred as an Honorary Doctor of Arts, the highest academic qualification in the UK, by the University of Bedfordshire in recognition of his services to literature.

Adam presents the regular crime fiction podcast *Partners in Crime* with fellow bestselling author and television actor Robert Daws.